Franco rowed them under the Bridge of Sighs, then through a narrow maze of canals.

As the light began to fade, Roberto switched to playing a mixture of ballads and short classical pieces. Gianni found himself relaxing, enjoying the views and the music and the changing colors in the sky.

When they went round a narrow corner, there was a slight jolt and somehow Gianni ended up with his arm around Serafina, steadying her on the seat.

Their eyes met, and color stole into her face. He could feel his own cheeks heating, too.

He wanted her. Really, really wanted her. Part of him remembered how it had felt to dance with her in St. Mark's Square and wanted to draw her closer, but part of him panicked, remembering how much he'd hurt after Elena had dumped him.

He withdrew his arm. "Safer than being on a roof, right?" he said drily.

But this wasn't a physical danger, one he knew how to minimize. It was an emotional danger, and he didn't know where to start guarding himself against that.

Dear Reader,

I fell in love with Venice on a water taxi, seeing
the city rising from the sea. I loved the crumbling
palazzos, the turquoise waters of the canal,
the bright pop of scarlet geraniums on ancient
windowsills and the beautiful stonework of the
bridges. So I really couldn't resist setting a book
there.

Add an impoverished *contessa* who doesn't believe
in love and needs to restore her ancestral home,
a builder who'd love to work on it but doesn't trust
himself not to fall for the wrong woman and a family
legend that turns out to have some unexpected
truths... I hope you enjoy Serafina and Gianni's
story, and have fun dancing under the moonlight
in St. Mark's Square with them—just as I had fun
dancing there with my husband and our then-small
children!

With love,

Kate Hardy

One Week in Venice with the CEO

Kate Hardy

—

HARLEQUIN®

Romance™

Recycling programs for this product may not exist in your area.

ISBN-13: 978-1-335-40701-6

One Week in Venice with the CEO

Copyright © 2022 by Pamela Brooks

Harlequin Enterprises ULC
22 Adelaide St. West, 41st Floor
Toronto, Ontario M5H 4E3, Canada
www.Harlequin.com

Printed in U.S.A.

Kate Hardy has been a bookworm since she was a toddler. When she isn't writing Kate enjoys reading, theater, live music, ballet and the gym. She lives with her husband, student children and their spaniel in Norwich, England. You can contact her via her website: katehardy.com.

Books by Kate Hardy

Harlequin Romance

For Gerard—one day we'll go back to Venice...

CHAPTER ONE

'If I could have a superpower,' Serafina said, 'I'd go back in time and visit every single Conte Ardizzone and persuade them to actually *fix* the problem instead of shutting off a room whenever there was a problem. And also,' she added wryly, 'stop them selling off the family silver when funds got low and then spending the proceeds on partying instead of sorting out the palazzo.'

Alessia winced. 'It's that bad?'

'It's that bad,' Serafina confirmed.

'Perhaps I should be giving you gin instead of coffee,' Alessia said.

Serafina shook her head. 'There aren't any real answers in the bottom of a gin glass, especially at ten o'clock in the morning. But coffee and a sugar rush would be wonderful.'

'Now *that* I can do. Sit down.' Alessia waved to the kitchen table, then busied herself with the expensive bean-to-cup machine Serafina usually teased her best friend about but was seriously grateful for right now.

Since her father's death, six months ago, Serafina had had to sort out the funeral and the endless admin, and then there had been the shock of finding out that the family trust fund was empty. And she was still having trouble getting her head round the reason *why* it was empty.

This morning's meeting at the bank had made it just that little bit worse.

While the coffee was brewing, Alessia took the lid off the jar containing *bussolai*, the ring-shaped lemon cookies that were a local speciality. 'Not another word until you've eaten three.'

The first cookie helped a bit. As did the second. By the third, Serafina could feel the sugar firing her up. 'You definitely have the magic touch, Lessi,' she said with a smile. 'Thank you.'

'Nonna's recipe never fails,' Alessia said. 'I'm assuming the bank isn't going to help?'

'No income equals no loan. And they've made it clear that even a solid business plan with projected income isn't good enough,' Serafina said. 'Bottom line: I still owe a chunk of the inheritance tax, and the only real asset I have right now is the palazzo itself. Which I can't sell, because it's entailed.' And now she was officially Contessa Serafina Ardizzone, the entailment meant that the palazzo was *her* problem. 'I can't rent it out or use it for any kind of business, because right now I'm pretty sure it'd fail every single health and safety directive going; but I can't afford to fix the problems, either.' She shook her head in mingled sadness and exasperation. 'If I'd had any idea about the state of the palazzo and our family finances when I was eighteen, I would've read law or economics instead of History of Art and picked a career that could support the palazzo. Or even become apprenticed to a builder who specialised in restoration, so I could all spend my spare time repairing the damage. Ten years of working on the place might've made enough of a difference.' She grimaced. 'But instead I thought the family money meant I didn't have to worry and I could study what I loved. Which makes me as bad as all the great-whatever-grandparents partying.'

In her case the partying had been with movie stars in Hollywood rather than with rich nobles in Venice; but it had ended with a broken heart. Hers.

And now the rest of her life had fractured, too.

Strictly speaking, she could walk away and let whoever inherited the palazzo from her deal with the problems, uncaring that the mouldering and neglect would get worse with every year. But that wasn't who Serafina was. She didn't dump her problems on other people, and she wasn't a quitter.

Plus she loved her house.

Which meant she was the one who needed to fix things.

'You're being unfair on yourself. You make it sound as if you've idled away the last decade, and that's not true. You've worked at the Museum of Women's Art as a volunteer ever since you did your Master's, and you've spent two years on the board. You have transferable skills,' Alessia said. 'You can look at something, see the business opportunity, persuade others to make changes, and write a grant application that actually gets mon—' She stopped mid-sentence. 'Can you apply for a grant to restore the palazzo?'

'Sadly not. You need something special to make a case for getting a restoration grant,' Serafina said. 'There are dozens of crumbling fifteenth-century palazzos in Venice, and Ca' d'Ardizzone doesn't have amazing architectural features, frescos or anything else to make it stand out from the others.'

'What about the Canaletto in your drawing room? If you put it up for auction, surely it would go for enough to pay for the repairs?'

'It would,' Serafina agreed, 'if it wasn't a copy.'

Alessia's eyes widened in shock. 'It's a *copy*?'

Serafina nodded. 'Apparently my great-great-great-grandfather sold the original. The same goes for the family jewellery: the originals were sold off over the years, and what we have now are paste copies that are practically worthless. I could try putting the porcelain up for auction, but what it would raise would barely make a dent in the debts.' She frowned. 'Maybe my dad was right. Maybe there really is a curse on the family. If my great-however-many-times-aunt Marianna had been allowed to marry the man she loved, three centuries ago, she wouldn't have tried to elope, fallen down the stairs and broken her neck—and he wouldn't have cursed the family.'

Alessia shivered. 'That's so sad. But of course there isn't a curse. Curses aren't real.'

Intellectually, Serafina knew that was true; but deep down she wondered if there was something in the story. Apparently Marianna's lover had declared, 'No Conte Ardizzone will have a happy marriage.' And, from what Serafina could see, that was precisely what had happened over the centuries. In her own lifetime, her grandparents had lived in different wings of the palazzo and refused to see each other. Her mother had turned into a bundle of nerves who only ever saw doom and gloom, and her father had become a gambling addict. Further back, the rumours were that her great-grandparents and great-great-grandparents had had difficult marriages: all the partying meant they hadn't had to spend time together.

And then there was her own near miss: she was relieved she'd discovered Tom in bed with another woman before she'd been foolish enough to marry him. Particularly as she'd learned later that it hadn't even been the first time he'd cheated on her. It seemed her movie star fiancé had wanted the cachet of marrying a Venetian countess; he'd been a good enough actor for Serafina to believe that he'd loved her for herself, when he'd only wanted her for her social position.

She'd fallen for his charm. Let him sweep her off her feet. Thought she'd be the first one in her family for decades to get her happy-ever-after with the man she loved...

Though she'd never make that mistake again. Not now she knew Tom hadn't really loved her.

She shook herself. 'I know you're right. There's been a long line of people who lived in the glory of the past and either didn't notice the present changing round them or refused to see it.' She took another gulp of coffee. 'But I wish my dad had said something to me years ago instead of struggling on his own. I wish I'd known we were broke. I wish I'd explored all the shut-off rooms properly and realised that "economising on the heating bills" was a euphemism for ignoring the real problems.'

'Maybe your dad didn't want to burden you,' Alessia suggested.

'But I'm his only child, Lessi. If he couldn't lean on me, who else could he have leaned on?' Not her mother, obviously. Francesca Ardizzone would've gone straight into catastrophe mode. But why hadn't he trusted her? That stung. Badly. 'If I'd known how bad things were, if I'd had any idea he was gambling with serious money and not just for centimes and a laugh with his friends, I could've—well, at least have tried to stop him. And then he wouldn't have had that last enormous loss and that heart attack.' And then he'd still be alive...

'Serafina, your dad's heart attack wasn't your fault,' Alessia said gently. 'It wasn't anyone's fault. Even if your dad hadn't lost that money, he might still have had a heart attack. You know how it is: stubborn middle-aged men who like their pastries a little too much, don't do any exercise and won't listen to any advice. My dad's the same. And every single one of my uncles. It's the way that generation is.'

Serafina knew it was true, but it didn't stop her feeling guilty. Or alone. Or mixed up: angry that her dad had been reckless and left her to clean up his mess, and hurt that he'd kept it all from her. He'd moved investments from the trust fund, hoping to beat the market, and got it wrong: and then he'd borrowed money from the fund to win back his losses. Except he'd lost again. And again. And again. The trust fund was empty, so Serafina and her mum had been living off her savings for the last six months. And the money was running out.

She squared her shoulders. There was no time

for moping. She needed to act. 'I need to make some money to fix the palazzo—or at least to fix enough of it to let me start making money from it, and the profits from that can go to fixing the next bit.' She raked a hand over her hair. 'The problems go back decades. They can't be fixed overnight, but I don't have to do everything at once. The first stage is to sort out some rooms to offer bed and breakfast, even if it's only a single suite to begin with. But what makes Ca' d'Ardizzone stand out from all the other ancient palazzos offering tourist accommodation? What's my USP?'

'You, of course,' Alessia said with a smile. 'How many other palazzos can offer *colazione con la contessa*?'

'Love the alliteration.' Serafina smiled back. 'And breakfast with a countess is definitely going to attract one particular segment of the market. But most guests are going to want more than that.'

'Painting lessons? You could run a retreat for painters, or for people who want to learn to paint. And where better to paint than overlooking the Grand Canal?'

'The view from my balcony's perfect,' Serafina agreed, 'but I've never taught anyone to paint.'

'But you could. Your watercolours are beautiful.'

'I paint for fun. For me,' Serafina said. 'Looking at it practically, I can't earn enough from art to pay the bills. And I need to keep something in my life that's just for me. Something to keep me sane.' Not that she'd ever admit it, even to her best friend, but something to fill up the empty spaces.

'OK. You've spent years working in an art museum and you know Venice like the back of your hand,' Alessia said. 'Maybe instead of art weekends, you can offer history of art weekends. Take your guests on a tour, and teach them about Venice and art.'

'That could work,' Serafina agreed. 'But first I need to get enough of the building up to standard, so people can actually stay at the palazzo. At the very least they'll want an en-suite bathroom, and renovations like that will cost money I don't have. The fact I need to take in paying guests at all makes it very clear I don't have any money. Nobody will agree to do the work on credit.' She sighed and took another biscuit. 'I almost wish I'd married Tom after all.'

'What?' Alessia looked shocked. 'But he cheated on you, Serafina. You would've been miserable with him.'

With a man who loved her title rather than her. 'I know. But Celebrity Life offered us a small fortune to run an exclusive on our wedding photos. I could've used money that to finance the ren—' Serafina stopped and snapped her fingers. 'That's it. You're right. *I*'m the USP.' She stood up and paced round Alessia's tiny kitchen. 'I know Tom was the movie star, but a Venetian countess would draw in the magazine's readers, too. The whole romance of Venice and an ancient palazzo—which, if we window-dress it and shoot in soft light, will look chic instead of shabby—and a society bride. If I marry someone who wants a society bride and we do an exclusive deal with the magazine over the wedding photos, I can use that money to restore the palazzo.'

Alessia shook her head. 'That's crazy, Serafina. It means marrying someone you don't love.'

No Conte Ardizzone will have a happy marriage.

Serafina shook herself. It was a myth, she reminded herself. Even if there was an awful lot of evidence in the unhappy marriages of her forebears to suggest it might be true. 'It won't be a permanent marriage. It'll be a marriage of convenience to suit us both, with a quiet divorce a year later. We both get what we want, nobody's hurt, and everybody's happy.' They didn't even have to live together: just make enough of a nuptial show to get the money for the photographs.

'Money—even if you're going to use that money to restore the palazzo rather than finance a lifestyle of partying—is *completely* the wrong reason to get married,' Alessia said. 'How about setting up a crowdfunding thing where people "buy a brick" or something and get a certificate for it saying that they've helped in the restoration of a Venetian palazzo? Bigger donors get something extra—once you've sorted out the accommodation, they can come and stay for a weekend of luxury.'

'That sort of thing works for public buildings,' Serafina said, 'but not for private homes. If I sell one brick at a time, it could take years to raise the money. In the meantime, the palazzo will decay that little bit more every day, and the renovation costs will grow—and probably at a faster rate than the donations come in.'

'Or maybe you could find a building company that would agree to staged payments in arrears, plus a discount, in return for publicity,' Alessia said. 'I did that feature for the Sunday supplement of La Cronaca last summer—the guy in Rome who took over his dad's construction company a couple of years back. He was looking at moving away from new builds and increasing their restoration work.' She looked thoughtful. 'Gianni Leto. I liked him. He was a bit intense, but he struck me as the reliable sort. Maybe you could talk to him. Working on a project like your palazzo would be good publicity for him. That puts you in a good bargaining position, because we can place features on the palazzo and its restoration. We can definitely get something in the lifestyle and travel magazines. If we're clever, we might be able to get a documentary out of it, too.'

They were more much practical ideas than her marriage of convenience, Serafina thought. Because who would want a temporary marriage to a penniless aristocrat who owned a money pit of a palazzo? And she had nothing to lose by asking Gianni Leto if he'd let her make staged payments. The worst-case scenario was that he'd say no, which left her in the same position as she was in now.

In the meantime, she needed to find a job with enough of a salary to pay the bills; working at the museum and giving all her time for nothing wasn't something she could afford to do any more. Not now the trust fund was empty. Though leaving the museum she loved so much was going to hurt. Badly. 'OK. Can you text me his details?'

'Sure. I'll do that now. And I'll email you the final press cutting and my notes, to give you his full background,' Alessia said.

Serafina hugged her. 'Thank you. And thank you for feeding me *bussolai* and listening to me whinge.'

'You're welcome to the cookies, and you weren't whinging. You're in a tough position and you need to bounce ideas off someone,' Alessia said. 'I still reckon you should set up a gin palazzo. It'd be perfect. You could have one of your pen-and-ink sketches of the palazzo on the label. Offer different flavours. For special editions, you could have bottles with Murano glass stoppers. You could do a deal with one of the glassmakers to offer exclusive hand-blown gin glasses. And the *pezzo forte*,' she said, flourishing one hand in the air, 'you can combine it with your B&B to offer gin-tasting weekends. Even gin-making weekends.'

'I love the idea,' Serafina said. 'Years ago, the ground floor of the palazzo would've been used as a warehouse. We have enough space for manufacture and storage. But gin-making means a distillery.'

'Not if you make bathtub gin,' Alessia said.

Serafina grinned. 'Now, who was it who did that feature on gin, made me go taste-testing with her and complained all the way through about the colour and taste of bathtub gin?' She sobered. 'To make a good, high-end gin, I'll need to buy equipment and employ a good distiller. Which means spending money, not to mention all the regulations about working environments—which *also* means spending money. And money's the thing I don't have.' She spread her hands. 'Until the palazzo's fixed, everything's a pipe dream. My ancestors' living in a dream world instead of facing reality is why I'm in trouble now, and it's my job to fix it. I'll start by talking to your builder.'

She swallowed hard. 'And getting a paid job. I know Madi can't afford to pay me a salary, so I'm going to have to resign. But I'll sign up with all the employment agencies and contact everyone I know who might be able to offer me a job.' She wasn't going to let the situation defeat her. It felt daunting, but she intended to rise to the challenge.

And she was going to win.

Later that afternoon, Serafina read the interview and notes from Alessia. Gianni Leto came across as a man who wasn't afraid of hard work, and who saw traditions as something to be cherished but also to be questioned. He didn't seem to be the sort who pushed change for change's sake: but he definitely came across as one who would consider a different approach if it would give a better result, rather than being hidebound by the way things had always been done.

She could work with that.

And maybe, as her best friend had suggested, she could talk him into giving her a discount and letting her make staged payments in exchange for helping him with publicity.

The next page was a portrait of him. The moody lighting made him look like a film star. Dark hair, cut short, dark, intense eyes and the most beautiful mouth she'd ever seen.

She shook herself. What Gianni Leto looked

like was completely irrelevant. She was more interested in his professional abilities. She'd been licking her wounds since Tom's betrayal, but sorting out things following her father's death and shouldering the burden of the palazzo meant that she didn't have time in her life for relationships in any case. Plus, for all she knew, he was already involved with someone.

Half an hour's searching on the internet told her that Gianni was definitely taking the family business in a new direction. His late father had done a lot of work with concrete, which had a massive carbon footprint; Gianni was looking to turn the company fully carbon neutral. And he was working on restoring properties rather than building new ones, using traditional materials where he could and new technology where it was appropriate. That boded well for him being interested in restoring the palazzo.

The company, under Gianni's direction, had paid for the restoration of the town hall in Bardicello two years ago. It seemed his father had built the hall from steel and concrete twenty years before; when part of the hall collapsed, there had been a massive scandal. Given the new direction of the firm, Gianni was clearly still trying to live that down. And perhaps, she thought, he was trying to restore his family's good name. Just as she needed to do—not that her dad had had a bad name, but if anyone learned about what he'd done with the family money then the gossip pages would have a field day.

Serafina had been focusing on Gianni Leto's professional life, but her search had also thrown up the fact that he was single. And he was focused entirely on his business, the same way she was focused on hers.

And maybe, just maybe, they could help each other by the plan that had horrified her best friend.

Marriage to a Venetian countess would give Gianni Leto social cachet and help to bury the scandal in his family's past. Marriage to him— provided she could persuade him into the photograph deal—would give her the funds she needed. He could restore the palazzo, giving him professional kudos. And she could pay for it, using the photograph money to start with and then doing the rest with money from the business.

They'd be able to give each other what they needed.

And then they could quietly part ways. Nobody got hurt. Everybody won.

Though this was a deal she wanted to suggest in person rather than on paper. First, she needed to set up a meeting.

Smiling, she switched into her email programme and began to write.

* * *

A business proposition from Contessa Serafina Ardizzone?

Gianni frowned. Didn't people of her class usually have someone to handle their business affairs, rather than doing it themselves?

But then he scrolled down to the first photograph and caught his breath.

The snap had clearly been taken from either the water or the opposite side of the canal, and showed a gorgeous four-storey Venetian palazzo. Fifteenth-century, he judged, a mix of gothic and Byzantine architecture. The stucco was painted deep pink; the white windows had stunning ogee arches; and there was a balcony running across the middle two storeys. He'd bet that the interior had amazing glass chandeliers and traditional Venetian terrazzo marble flooring. And the ceilings—at the very least there would be beautiful beams. There might also be frescos or intricate decorative plasterwork, things he itched to work with.

The next photograph showed the interior of one of the rooms. Exactly as he'd expected: traditional terrazzo flooring, flexible enough to move with the building. High ceilings. It looked as if they were wooden, rather than painted, but they were still gorgeous. Antique glass chandeliers. And damask wall-coverings—he zoomed in closer—that definitely showed signs of damp around the windows; it was obvious there were leaks. The rest of the interior photographs showed more of the same. Some of the floors appeared to be parquet; it was possible they'd been laid to cover up problems with the flooring beneath it.

The palazzo was the kind of building Gianni would give his eye teeth to work on: one that clearly hadn't been touched for decades, apart from the installation of electricity and maybe some plumbing, and even that had probably been decades ago.

But why was the Contessa asking someone from Rome to do the restoration, rather than someone local?

He scrolled down past the rest of the photographs to her short email.

I've recently inherited Ca' d'Ardizzone and it needs some restoration work. My best friend, Alessia da Campo, interviewed you last year for La Cronaca, and she suggested that this might be your area of expertise. If you'd be interested in tendering for the job, perhaps we could meet at your office in Rome to discuss options.

Gianni remembered the interview very well. The journalist had done her research beforehand, asked intelligent questions, and written a fair and balanced piece. If Serafina Ardizzone was her best friend, then he was happy to listen to what she had to say.

But it still nagged at him that the countess hadn't turned to a local firm. In his experience, that usually meant a lack of trust somewhere. Either she'd been ripped off before and wanted a personal recommendation, or her family were known locally for not paying their bills on time—if at all—and nobody would advance her credit.

Wondering which it was, he flicked into the internet and looked her up.

Contessa Serafina Ardizzone was the only child of the late Conte Marco Ardizzone and Contessa Francesca Ardizzone. There were photographs of her parents: her mother glittering in diamonds and designer dresses and her father in old-fashioned evening dress, attending opening nights at the opera and gallery previews. Since the palazzo bore her family name, they'd obviously lived in Venice for centuries. It was clear that she came from an aristocratic and cultured background: the complete opposite of his own. He preferred rock to opera, loathed the pretentious squiggles that people called modern art, and his family had been desperately poor when he was young and his father had been out of work.

Another story reported that her father had died six months ago from a heart attack. He knew how it felt to lose a parent that way; though whether Serafina had had as tempestuous a relationship with her father as he'd had with his own, he had no idea.

There were more photographs of Serafina in her role as a board member of the Museum of Women's Art, wearing a designer suit and incredibly cute specs. He added 'bright' to his list; no charitable foundation could afford to have a board member who didn't pull their weight, however pretty she might be. And Serafina Ardizzone was extremely pretty. Dark hair that framed her heart-shaped face in ringlets, huge dark eyes, and a wide smile that would have any man falling to his knees at her feet. She looked like a movie star.

Which wasn't far from the truth, as the next story showed Serafina with her arms wrapped round Tom Burford, one of the most popular action movie heroes. Tom's blond hair was a perfect foil to her dark beauty. It seemed they were Hollywood's golden couple and the photo had been taken at their engagement party a year ago. Though, even if Serafina been single, Gianni didn't have the time for a relationship. Or the inclination, since his break-up with Elena. In her family's view, his money had made up for the fact he came from a lower-class background and worked in a trade, and they'd just about been able to tolerate an engagement. But when the problems with the town hall came to light they'd been very quick to distance themselves from him. Elena herself had dumped him a couple of days later, and her lack of faith in him had broken something inside him. Maybe his heart; maybe his faith in himself, too. He'd thought she'd loved him, though clearly he'd deluded himself.

He'd learned from Elena that posh women were trouble: and a *contessa* was beyond posh.

He shook himself. This wasn't about him. This was about a job. Restoring a palazzo. To be part of the Hollywood elite meant that you had money; funding the restoration obviously wouldn't be a problem. And he knew he'd love the work. Part of him itched to email back and say straight away that he'd do it.

But.

Could he work with her? Would she trust his professional judgement and let him get on with his job? Or would she be forever asking questions and irritating him? The Hollywood photos and her aristocratic background suggested she might be a little snobby; but that story about her work with the art museum and the fact she was best friends with a journalist he'd liked suggested that maybe she'd be good to work with.

There was only one way to find out.

The best way.

Face to face. Where nobody could hide.

He replied to her email, suggesting three dates for a meeting the following week.

And then he'd find out exactly what her proposition entailed.

'Serafina!' Maddalena, the museum director, greeted her with a warm hug. 'I'm glad you're in today. You're the person I want to see most in the entire world, right now.'

She wouldn't be, once Serafina gave her the news.

But, before Serafina could tell her, Maddalena said, 'I've never thought of myself as a violent person, but I could cheerfully strangle Beppe Russo.' Beppe was the CEO of the company that had bought the building housing the museum.

'What's he done now?' Serafina asked.

'The lease renewal,' Maddalena said. 'I've nagged and nagged and *nagged* him for the paperwork.' She banged a hand on her desk. 'I finally got it this morning. No wonder he dragged his feet about handing it over. He's quadrupling the cost of the lease.'

'What?' Serafina stared at her in shock.

'We can't cover the extra costs. We can't even begin to cover them. And he knows it.'

'He can't quadruple the rent, Madi.'

'Oh, yes, he can. He owns the building. Our lease runs out in three months. He can do what the hell he likes, and he knows it.' Maddalena's hands balled into fists. 'Either we suck up the extra costs—which he knows we can't do—or we find somewhere else. And it's obvious he's banking on the latter, so he can gut the building and turn this place into a hotel.' She shook her head. 'But finding a new home within our budget… I'm definitely going to need you and your skills.'

How could Serafina possibly resign now?

And yet—how could she not?

Maddalena looked at her. 'Say something, *carissima*. You're the one with all the great ideas.'

If her palazzo hadn't been crumbling away, Serafina would've known exactly where the museum could move to.

Or maybe…

'Madi, can I tell you something in strictest confidence?' Serafina asked.

'Of course.'

'I was coming to see you to resign.'

'Resign? Oh, no.' Maddalena frowned. 'Why, *carissima*? You love it here—and we love you. Has someone upset you? If it's Beppe, I'll go and rearrange his—'

'Not Beppe,' Serafina cut in hastily. 'The problem is, the palazzo's falling to bits and it needs a lot of work doing to it—which costs money—plus I still owe a chunk of the inheritance tax.' Her father's gambling habit had done even more damage to their finances, but nobody else needed to know that. 'I love it here, but I need a job that pays the bills, and I know you can't afford to pay me.'

'I don't want to lose you. If that weasel Beppe hadn't dumped this on me, I would've found the money from *somewhere* to pay you a salary,' Maddalena said, scowling. 'Which is another good reason to strangle him.'

'If my palazzo didn't need renovating, you could've moved the museum to the ground floor and not had to worry about paying rent,' Serafina said. 'It's not as big as the space we have here, but we could maybe have temporary extra exhibitions in the ballroom, or in the *portego* on the *piano nobile*.'

The women looked at each other.

'I think we could solve each other's problems, *carissima*,' Maddalena said. 'We could pay you the same rent as we pay here. That would help you with the bills, wouldn't it?'

'I can't ta—' Serafina began, horrified at the idea of taking money from the museum she wanted to support.

'Rent is a running cost,' Maddalena cut in. 'And I'd much rather pay the rent to you than to someone like Beppe.'

Serafina thought about it. The rent would help her pay the bills. Having the museum on the ground floor meant that the house would be used properly again, full of people instead of ghosts. And she wouldn't have to resign from the job she loved.

But, given the situation with the museum's lease, it also meant she'd need to get the ground floor fixed within three months. She didn't have the money to pay for it, and the museum couldn't afford to pay her a year's rent in advance.

'Please don't resign,' Maddalena said. 'Let the museum rent your ground floor. It works for both of us. And we'll all come and help do whatever we can with the restoration in our spare time— paint walls, grout tiles, clean, fetch and carry, whatever.'

A team effort.

Saving the museum, saving the palazzo, and making life better for all of them.

Could they do it?

'I'll speak to the guy I'm hoping will assess the palazzo,' Serafina said. 'If he says the ground floor can be fixed in three months, then it's yours.'

And for the first time in months she felt a flicker of hope.

CHAPTER TWO

ROME. THE ETERNAL CITY. Serafina had loved her three years studying in the city, the way that you could turn the corner of a busy modern street and suddenly there would be ancient buildings right in front of you. She'd got used to the traffic rushing around instead of gondolas and motor boats and the water bus, and on days when she'd missed the canals of home she'd walked alongside the broad, fast-flowing Tiber, soothed by the water.

She walked past the Colosseum simply because it was her favourite building in the city and even the sight of it made her smile, and then she headed for Gianni Leto's office.

Surprisingly, it was all steel and glass. How could someone who was changing his firm's focus to the restoration of old buildings work in something that was the complete opposite?

But criticising him would only put his back up. And she needed to do a charm offensive to get him on her side—for the museum's sake as well as her own. Mentally preparing herself for the encounter, she walked up the stone steps, took the lift to the top floor and found the reception area for Leto Construction.

'Good afternoon,' she said to the receptionist with a smile. 'I'm Serafina Ardizzone, and I have a meeting scheduled with Signor Leto at two.'

'He's expecting you.' The receptionist smiled back. 'Let me show you through to his office.'

Gianni Leto's office was small but very neat. It was minimally furnished with a desk, a chair, a chair for visitors and a filing cabinet. The surface of his desk was clear except for a laptop and a mobile phone. The walls that weren't glass were painted magnolia, and a series of large photographs in black frames hung at intervals. Serafina presumed that the buildings in the photographs had either been constructed or restored by Leto Construction.

The man himself stood up as the receptionist ushered her in. 'Thank you for being prompt, Contessa.'

She didn't want her title to be a barrier. She needed this man on her side. 'I prefer to conduct business on first-name terms. Call me Serafina,' she said, holding her hand out to shake his. 'Thank you for seeing me, Signor Leto.'

'Gianni.'

The photograph from Alessia's article had been a moody shot and hadn't done him justice. He was beautiful enough that he could've been a model. And in the flesh he had more stage presence than any of the movie stars she'd met, including Tom.

His handshake was firm and businesslike, but the touch of his fingers against hers sent a zing all the way through her. It was hard not to look at that beautiful mouth and wonder what it might feel like against her skin.

Serafina shook herself mentally. This wasn't what their meeting was supposed to be about. This was about saving the palazzo and the museum. Nothing to do with attraction. Or sex.

'May I offer you some coffee, Serafina?' he asked. 'Or something cold?'

She needed to focus instead of letting herself dream about something she knew didn't even exist. 'Thank you, but no.'

He inclined his head. 'Then please have a seat.' He gestured to the chair in front of his desk.

She smiled and sat down.

Despite knowing Serafina Ardizzone's background, Gianni hadn't expected her to be quite so glamorous. Everything from her well-cut suit to her understated make-up screamed class and money. Old money. Old class—the sort that Elena's family had aspired to but hadn't quite managed.

But it was more than that: it was the woman herself.

Serafina was the first woman in years who'd made him feel as if an electric current ran through him when he shook her hand. It made him feel breathless and dizzy. Like a callow teenager. As if his tongue had been glued to the roof of his mouth.

Say something, he told himself. *Act, don't react.*

She was here because she wanted him to do a job for her. And he needed to remember that. Put the business first. It was obvious they should talk about the building. Hoping he sounded a lot calmer than he felt as he sat down again, he drawled, 'I understand you're looking at restoring the palazzo.'

She inclined her head. 'Which I know is going to take time and money.'

At least she was being realistic about some of it. Other parts, not so much. 'It's a long way between Rome and Venice,' he pointed out. Half the country. Five hundred kilometres, give or take. The journey between the two cities took more than three hours, even on a high-speed train.

'So why am I looking at contractors a long way from home?' she asked.

He liked the way she'd picked up on his concerns. 'It makes sense to use local contractors and reduce your carbon footprint. Particularly as Venice has unique challenges and local builders would know those issues and the best solutions in depth.'

'True.' She looked him in the eye. 'But I want the right person for the job, Gianni. Someone who will understand the building and its heritage, and do a sympathetic job.'

'I'd need to see the building for myself and judge the extent of the work before I can give you a quote,' he said. 'Has any work been done on the foundations?'

'I have no idea. There's no paperwork relating to any building work in the last four decades,' she said, 'and my father definitely didn't mention anything happening when he was a child. I assume the foundations are original. Though the wooden piles under Venetian buildings don't tend to rot as timber usually does, because they're covered in mud and then a layer of stone: meaning the oxygen and microbes that do the damage can't actually get to the wood.'

'But there's still *acqua alta*—' the high tides that sent floods sweeping through the city '—which are becoming more frequent every year,' he said. 'And the flooding's salt water. You didn't send me photographs of the side of the palazzo, but I'm guessing the stucco's come away and exposed the brickwork.'

'And there are visible salt deposits and that green line of algae,' she agreed, 'the same as with many other canalside buildings in the city.'

For someone who claimed to know nothing about architecture, Gianni thought, Serafina was remarkably well-informed. She knew about foundations, salt deposits and what made wood rot. He had a feeling there was more to this than met the eye.

She looked him straight in the eye. 'You restored the town hall in Bardicello.'

The building his father had constructed, where the steel inserts had eventually cracked the concrete and caused part of a wall to collapse. They were lucky nobody had been hurt. But the reputation of Leto Construction had suffered, even though Gianni had fixed the damage. He was still struggling to restore his father's good name.

She clearly knew the worst. Did she plan to use it as leverage? 'And restoring the palazzo would be good publicity for my company, so you think we'll offer to do the job cheaply?' he asked coolly.

'No. It means you'll do the job well because you'll be mindful of your reputation.'

That warmed him; but at the same time it put him on his guard. 'And the rest of it?'

She looked at him, as if calculating something. 'I need to restore the palazzo.'

He already knew that. 'And how do you plan to use the building? Are you looking to make it into apartments or a hotel? Use part of it for some kind of business?' When she said nothing, he said, 'You'll need to make decisions about the restoration before any work starts, and what you plan to do with the palazzo will obviously affect those decisions.'

'At the moment, my mother and I live on the *piano nobile*,' she said.

The first floor. Gianni knew this was where the aristocratic owners had entertained guests and kept their private apartments; some palazzos had a second *piano nobile*. The ground floor of a Venetian palazzo had traditionally been used for business or warehousing, and the servants had been housed in the hidden top floor.

'The house is way too big for the two of us. And I'm not prepared to let the palazzo simply rot away while Mamma and I inhabit a few rooms,' she said. 'I want the building brought back to life. Used, instead of mouldering away.'

'Assuming that most of the rooms are in the same state as those in the photographs you sent me, it's likely to take time and money,' he said. 'There will be mess—a lot of mess—and a lot of noise. I'll be honest with you: your best option would be to sell it to a developer, The sort who has a conscience and wants to do things properly, and will either turn the palazzo into an upmarket hotel, or maybe strip it back and turn it into luxury apartments.'

She looked at him as if he'd offered her a dish

of maggots, a mixture of disgust and disdain. 'I can't sell the palazzo. It's entailed.'

'You could rent it out.'

'Right now,' she said, 'it'd probably breach every health and safety regulation going. It's damp and it's crumbling. It needs renovating first. It's my palazzo, it's the fault of my ancestors that it's in the state it's in now, and it's my job to fix it.'

There was a hint of steel and fire in her eyes. He liked that. A lot. Serafina Ardizzone wouldn't back down when something seemed difficult at first glance. She was clearly the sort who'd look at the options and find a way to make things work. She'd push and she'd ask questions, because she wanted to understand the situation and do things properly. Gianni knew he'd enjoy working with someone who was that invested in a job.

Though he damped down the voice in his head that asked if he was more interested in her or in the job. This wasn't about fancying someone out of his league. It was about work.

'Bottom line, the building needs to earn its keep. I plan to rent the ground floor and maybe part of the first floor to a museum.' She spread her hands. 'I also want to use the ballroom on the floor where we live now. As well as exhibitions, we could hold banquets, serving food made from historical recipes; or we could hold musical evenings with the musicians wearing period costume and using period instruments. Or lectures with period refreshments. It'd be easy to fill the seats.'

Eating historical food and listening to a classical concert wasn't the sort of thing Gianni had ever considered doing, but Serafina's enthusiasm was infectious and he was surprised to discover that he was tempted to try both—if she was involved. She was so far away from his own world that she intrigued him. He wanted to know what made her tick; and to see things the way she saw them.

'I'd retain most of the first floor for my family's use, and in time I'd use the second and third floors as accommodation,' she said. 'Possibly for holiday lets, or possibly for longer-term tenancies. But to start with I need the ground floor restored to the point where it could be used by a museum, plus a couple of suites on the first floor that I could use for guests.'

'Restoration in stages,' he said thoughtfully. 'That's doable, provided you warn your guests that there will be noise and mess. But, whatever you plan to do, you need to look at the causes of the dampness first and fix it. Obviously I can't tell you what the causes and the best solutions are without seeing the place, but the options are likely to include tanking—that's putting in a waterproof membrane and concrete to elevate the ground floor above the flood-risk height—or fill-

ing the cavities in the wall with special material
so the salt water can't seep upwards. Then you
need to look at any other areas of the building
which are letting in water, and look at the heating and ventilation to deal with condensation.'

'Will that be expensive to fix? And will it take
long?'

'It depends what damage there is already,' he
said. 'As a rule of thumb, where restoration's concerned, always overestimate the cost by at least
fifty per cent. That way you'll avoid the worst of
the shocks.'

And now he had to do the bit that Elena's family had always thought vulgar. Mention money.
Would this be where she backed away, like they
would've done? 'In Venice, everything has to be
shipped in. Literally,' he said. 'It's going to cost
more than it would in a city where things can be
delivered by road. And some of those costs will
need to be paid up front.'

'Of course.' She inclined her head. 'Could we
perhaps agree staged payments?'

Staged payments? Did she mean that she needed
to have the work done first and rent out the ground
floor before she'd have enough money to pay his
bill? She'd made it clear that she needed the building to pay its way. It seemed that Contessa Serafina Ardizzone, despite her lifestyle—or maybe
because of it—didn't have very much in the bank.

'I'd still need a deposit,' he said carefully. 'As would any other contractor.'

'I'm not asking you to do the work for nothing,' she said. 'I'm proposing a business deal.'

Hadn't she done that already, by asking him to quote for a restoration job? He didn't understand what else she could mean.

'You and I,' she said, 'both have…difficulties, shall we say?'

He folded his arms, not liking the sound of this. 'Don't beat around the bush.'

'All right. What happened at Bardicello damaged your company's reputation. A high-profile project like restoring the palazzo will help people to forget that.' She took a deep breath. 'Plus my name will help you. And I have the contacts to get you excellent publicity. Definitely magazines, and possibly television.'

He didn't have a clue where she was going with this. 'What exactly are you suggesting?'

Marry me.

Though Serafina couldn't quite bring herself to say it. She knew her best friend was right: the marriage of convenience was a stupid idea. Who would marry a complete stranger? Of course he'd refuse.

But maybe if he got to know her—if he came to stay at the palazzo, to survey it, he might fall in love with the place. And then she could ask him; and then he might say yes.

'Do you know Venice, Gianni?' she asked instead.

He rolled his eyes. 'Everyone knows Venice. Canals, gondolas, masks, glass.'

It was what the tourists came to see; but there was much more to the city than that. 'When did you last visit the city?'

'I've never been,' he admitted.

'Then you know what everyone *thinks* Venice is, which isn't the same thing at all,' she said. 'Here's my proposal. Come and stay with me for a week. Look at the palazzo and tell me realistically what needs doing, how long it will take and how much it will cost. In return, you get to stay in a palazzo right on the Grand Canal—the best location anyone could ask for. Breakfast on the terrace, where you can watch the boats on the water while you sip your coffee. Mornings strolling around the *calle*, finding hidden treasures at every corner, with someone who can tell you their history and point out little details you might not have noticed. Lunch in a little courtyard filled with flowers, and the sound of birdsong and church bells everywhere instead of traffic. Dinner in a tiny restaurant with amazing food: a place where the locals eat and the menu's what the chef picked up at the market that morning. A glass of

wine on the terrace, watching the last streaks of
the sunset fade from the sky and the canal turning dark as night, the reflections from the lights
in the buildings looking like stars on the water.
It's heaven on earth.'

The picture she painted… Gianni could already
feel himself falling under the spell of Venice. And
under the spell of Serafina herself; he couldn't
remember the last time he'd actually noticed
the colour of a woman's eyes and the way they
changed with the light and her mood.

This was meant to be business, and he was trying to put the past to bed and rebuild his family's
good name. Letting himself get side-tracked by
the most beautiful woman he'd ever met, a woman
whose words spun fairy tales around him and
made the world glow, would be the worst thing
he could do.

He reframed her proposal into much plainer
language. 'You want me to survey the building
for nothing, and test market what you're offering
your guests?'

Colour tinged her cheeks. 'Not *quite*. I'm suggesting a kind of barter. A survey of the building
in return for a week's accommodation, food and
entertainment.'

'And the accommodation, food and entertainment is what you plan to offer your guests.'

She shook her head. 'They'll pay for their own lunch and dinner. You won't.'

'If I want to drink vintage champagne and eat lobster at the most expensive restaurant in Venice, that's OK with you?' he asked, guessing that it would be way outside her budget and wanting to see how far he could push her.

'Like a rich tourist, you mean? Then you won't be eating like a local,' she said crisply, 'which is what *I'm* offering.'

She thought on her feet, and she stood up for herself. The more she sparred with him, the more he wanted to get to know her. He wasn't used to being intrigued by someone and it flustered him slightly; at the same time, he found it irresistible.

'What you'll get,' she said, 'is a personal tour guide, good food, decent wine, and accommodation in an amazing location.'

'In a damp, crumbling palazzo,' he reminded her. Wasn't that the whole point? She lived in a house that was falling down. She'd already admitted that in its current state it'd breach every health and safety regulation going.

'Shabby chic is very trendy, is it not?' she asked. 'In my case it's also authentic. Furniture that's been in my family for years, not bought from a flea market and given a fake "distressed" paint job. That's a double win.'

He'd give her bonus point for that. On a sales

team, she'd be the outstanding star. She could put the perfect spin on things. No wonder the museum had snapped her up for their board. He'd bet she could talk people into sponsorship deals, or into lending them priceless works of art for an exhibition.

Her work, combined with her best friend, meant that she'd been truthful about having good press contacts. If he worked on her palazzo, he'd get excellent publicity. Something that would definitely make people forget Bardicello. He'd finally be able to restore his family's good name and hold his head up high. Be proud again instead of cautious.

Ah, who was he kidding? It wasn't the job that made him want to say yes. It wasn't even the prospect of working on the kind of building that made his heart sing. It was *her*. This clever, energetic woman who made everything around him feel as if the brightness had been turned up, pulling him out of the shadows.

Which was why he ought to say no.

She obviously didn't have the money to cover the restoration. She'd admitted she needed the house to pay for itself and she'd asked about stage payments. She was even bartering with him rather than paying up front for a survey, which was one of the cheapest items on a restoration job. Did she have any money at all?

His best guess was that she didn't.

From a business point of view, this was going to be an utter disaster. He shouldn't let his attraction to her blinker his common sense.

On the other hand, it was months since he'd taken a break. Probably years, if he was honest with himself; he hadn't been on holiday since his father had died.

A week in Venice, staying in the kind of building that fascinated him and doing the part of the job he loved most: looking at the house, seeing what needed doing, working out how to fix the problems while still staying true to the building's heart. Traditional craftsmanship mixed with modern ideas.

And he'd have his own personal tour guide: a good, solid reason to spend a bit more time with her.

How could he say no?

'All right. It's a deal. Show me your Venice, and I'll do a proper assessment of your house.'

Was it his imagination, or was that relief he could see in those dark, luminous eyes—albeit quickly masked?

'Thank you.' She took her phone out of her bag and flicked into what he assumed was her diary app when she said, 'When's convenient for you?'

It seemed that she was no slouch when it came to closing a deal, either.

Serafina Ardizzone might look like a movie star, but underneath she was an extremely astute businesswoman: one who knew better than to give him time to change his mind.

'I'll check my diary and get back to you,' he said, deliberately baiting her because he wanted to know what she'd do next and where she'd take this.

She glanced at her watch. 'We still have ten minutes left of our meeting. Let's take that window to check your diary. Especially as your laptop is right in front of you.'

Astute businesswoman? No, she was more like a shark pretending to be a mermaid. And he didn't care that he was mixing his metaphors.

The more he saw of Serafina Ardizzone, the more she drew him.

Serafina. Seraph. Angel.

Angels were supposed to be blonde and ethereal, weren't they? Serafina was dark and very, very real. Not in the least bit angelic. That mouth was pure temptation.

How could he possibly resist?

He opened his diary. 'A week.' He was busy. But he could delegate. It would probably be good for him to learn how to delegate, instead of insisting on knowing every single detail of every single project. His father's micro-management had driven him crazy; but here he was, if he was honest, doing exactly the same thing to his team. Gianni didn't want to turn into his father and stifle their creativity, the way his father had stifled him. Serafina Ardizzone had just given him the perfect excuse to loosen the reins a little. Or was he finding the perfect excuse to accept her offer?

'All right. Let's make it Monday.'

'Monday's fine. Will you arrive by train or plane?'

Normally, he'd drive. But Venice had canals rather than roads, so driving wasn't appropriate. 'Train. It's better for the environment than flying.'

She inclined her head. 'I'll meet you at the train station. What time?'

'Morning,' he said. 'I'll let you know the arrival time once I've booked my ticket.'

'Wonderful.' But her smile wasn't pure triumph. He couldn't quite read it, but he thought there might be a tinge of relief. 'Monday morning it is. Do you have any specific dietary requirements?'

'No.'

'And you're OK with fish?' she checked.

'I'm not fussy about food,' he said. Growing up poor meant either you ate what you were given, or you went hungry. He'd never lost the habit, even though nowadays he didn't have to worry about money.

She put a note in her diary. 'I'm sure you're busy. I won't waste your time by chattering on about nothing.' She stood up and proffered her hand. 'Thank you for your time. I'll see you on Monday.'

Again, when he shook her hand, Gianni's skin tingled. So did his mouth. He was going to have to work on that and get his reaction under control before Monday. 'Monday,' he said, and hoped she hadn't heard the slight croak in his voice.

'*Ciao,*' she said, and gave him a smile that sent his pulse rate up several notches.

And then she sashayed out of his office.

Oh, dear God. What had he let himself in for?

But a smile tugged at the corner of his mouth as he checked what he needed to move and what he needed to delegate.

Serafina kept the bright smile fixed on her face as she thanked the receptionist, but in the lift her knees very nearly sagged.

Gianni Leto had actually agreed to the first part of her plan.

And it was only now that she realised she'd expected him to refuse.

He'd arrive on Monday. Today was Wednesday. That gave her less than a week to prepare.

But preparation was her strong suit. She was about to sit on a train for three hours. Three uninterrupted hours, when she had nothing else to do but focus on Gianni Leto and how to get him to fall in love with Venice and the palazzo. And then maybe she could persuade him to take that one tiny step and marry her, temporarily. That would give her the money to pay him. And then she could rescue both the museum and the palazzo.

She bought a double espresso from one of the kiosks in the station, found her seat, and took a pen and pad from her bag, ready to start making lists. At the planning stage, she preferred the old-fashioned way; there was a direct connection between her hand and her brain, plus later she could see ideas she'd deleted and possible revisit them or tweak them.

But, before she did that, there was something else important she needed to do: persuade her mother to go on holiday for a week. She didn't want her mother to know a thing about her plans for the palazzo until everything was agreed. Francesca took worry to an art form, and Serafina had learned very quickly to copy her father's habit of keeping everything vague, to stop her mother going into catastrophe mode.

Even though Serafina loved her mother dearly, part of her resented the fact that she had to tip-toe round her mother's sensitivities all the time. Weren't you supposed to be able to lean on your parents when things got tough? But, for as long as she could remember, it had been the other way round. She was the one who had to jolly Francesca along. The one who had to find the bright side. The supporter, not the leaner.

She squared her shoulders. That wasn't ever going to change, so it was pointless dwelling on it. Better to use her energy on something positive, the way she always did, instead of wallowing. She'd save the palazzo, save the museum and make sure that her mother didn't have to worry about a thing.

Which meant she needed to keep all the details to herself: though she was realistic enough to know that she wouldn't be able to do any of it without some help.

She took her phone from her bag and called her aunt.

'Serafina! How are you, *piccola*?'

'Very well, thank you. And you, Tia Vittoria?'

'I'm about to head off to aqua aerobics, but I always have time for my favourite niece.'

She was Vittoria's only niece, just as Vittoria was her only aunt, but the affection was real and made Serafina feel warm inside. 'Good. Tia Vittoria, may I ask a huge, huge favour from you?'

'Of course.'

'I have someone coming to see the palazzo next week. To assess it, then tell me what the problems are and what can be done to fix them. And I don't want Mamma worrying herself sick about it.'

'Plus you don't need Cesca in doom-and-gloom mode, talking to your assessor and giving him all the worst-case scenarios,' Vittoria said. 'Which you, *piccola*, are too loyal to say, but she's my little sister so *I* can say it. It can be the brightest, sunniest day, and your mother will still find the clouds and rain.'

It was true; and it was incredibly wearing, trying to make someone see the bright side when their natural inclination was gloom, gloomier and gloomiest. 'Even agreeing with you makes me feel like a really horrible person,' Serafina said, guilt prickling through her veins.

Because you weren't supposed to be mean about your family. You were supposed to love them unconditionally.

Even when you weren't totally sure they loved you back.

No, that wasn't fair. Her mother *did* love her. It just got a bit lost under all the misery.

'You're not horrible at all,' Vittoria said. 'But we need to be practical here and work round the obstacles. Let me know when the survey is, and I'll take Cesca out for a very long lunch and then make her help me find a new dress or something until the assessor's gone.'

'That's lovely of you,' Serafina said. 'But I'm afraid it's not going to be for only a day.'

'The palazzo's that bad?'

'I think it might be,' Serafina admitted. 'But I have a plan.' She told her aunt about the museum's plight, about the deal she'd reached with Gianni, and how she intended to raise the money to fix the ground floor.

'Firstly,' Vittoria said, 'a marriage of convenience is a *terrible* idea. I know Tom hurt you and the way he cheated on you stopped you believing in love, but it does exist.'

'I'm not so sure it does, for my family. Look at my parents and my grandparents. They weren't happy together, but they stuck it out because everyone expected it of them. And I'm guessing it was the same back in the nineteenth century, and the century before that.' Serafina sighed. 'Maybe the family curse is real.'

'That curse is a family story to explain away bad behaviour,' Vittoria said briskly. 'Your grandparents were of a different generation— and they were toxic. Your parents should have moved out instead of staying at the palazzo, and your father needed a proper job instead of being a count in waiting. Living with difficult in-laws and being dependent on them for money is a recipe for misery. It's no wonder that things turned out the way they did.'

Serafina knew her aunt had a point. If her father had had something to fulfil him and a place of his own, he might not have started gambling to keep himself occupied. And her mother might have been more like Vittoria, finding the joy instead of the shadows everywhere she looked. Serafina had been determined not to let herself be dragged down in the same way, and she'd always managed to find a positive for every situation.

'And now there's you,' Vittoria said. 'Bright, clever, beautiful you. You deserve a partner who'll support you and let you shine, Serafina. A partner who'll love you all the way back.'

Which, so far, hadn't happened. 'Let's agree to disagree on that one, Tia Vittoria,' Serafina said. 'I don't want the headache of a husband.' Except possibly for a convenient one. 'But the rest of it? Can you help me?'

'If your assessor falls in love with Venice and the palazzo, then I agree he's more likely to help you. He's in the business of structures rather than their contents; he might know about grants that you don't,' Vittoria said. 'Of course I'll help you. I'll call your mother tonight and ask her to come and stay with me for a week, because I miss my little sister and I want to spend some time with her.' She paused. 'I'll say want to replant some of the borders and I need her to help me with the research. We'll need to go and visit several gardens and have lunch out. She'll enjoy that.'

Serafina wasn't sure her mother enjoyed anything other than finding the gloomy spots, nowadays. A disloyal part of her thought her mother rather enjoyed having the excuse of widowhood so she could be ostentatiously miserable. Serafina missed her dad, but she'd buried her grief by keeping herself busy. On the other hand, she needed to know exactly what they were facing with the restoration so she could put it in a kinder form for her mother, and that meant getting Francesca away from the palazzo while Gianni assessed it. 'Thank you. I owe you. Massively.'

'I'm happy to help,' Vittoria said. 'I wish I could do more. I have some savings; they won't make much of a dent in restoring that monstrosity of a palazzo, but you're welcome to them if it will help.'

Serafina swallowed hard. 'That's really kind, but I can't take your money.'

'Better to have it now, when it can be useful, than wait until I die—because I intend to live to at least a hundred and be one of these old women who terrifies the entire village,' Vittoria said. 'And now I must go, *piccola*, or I'll be late for class.' She chuckled. 'Make sure Cesca packs her swimming costume. I'll take her with me next week. She'll be too busy following the moves to worry about anything.'

Once she'd said goodbye to her aunt, Serafina felt much lighter of heart.

How did you make someone fall in love with a city?

She made of list of places to take Gianni: places where the food was good, or where the buildings were stunning. At this time of year, it was a little quieter; she could take him to see the Doge's Palace and the Basilica when the square wasn't completely teeming with people. And she could take him to lesser-known spots, too; she was pretty sure he'd love the spiral staircase on the outside of the Palazzo Contarini del Bovolo.

La Serenissima in spring.

It was her favourite time of year, when it was warm enough that you didn't need a coat but cool enough that you could walk all day without needing to find a patch of shade to collapse in. Wisteria tumbling from walls, blossom on the trees, and terracotta pots stuffed with greenery and pops of colour to dress windows, bridges and terraces. It was the time of year when she spent the most time painting, loving the beauty of her city and wanting to capture it in watercolours. She wouldn't have to do much; the city would do the work for her and make Gianni fall in love.

She'd just about finished her lists when the

train pulled in to Venice. She caught the *vaporetto* to the Rialto, picked up a bouquet of bright pink peonies for her mother from her favourite florist, then walked through the back streets to the back door of the palazzo.

Her footsteps echoed in the hall as she crossed to the stairs.

'I'm going to fix you,' she whispered, stroking the marble newel post. 'You're going to shine again. Especially when the museum moves here. But you need to help me, so I can help you and help the museum. You need to make Gianni Leto fall in love with you, the way I love you.'

And she was definitely going crazy, talking to her house.

She shook herself. Now to face her mother. She took a deep breath, reminded herself to smile, and headed up to the sitting room overlooking the canal. If her mother was reading or doing something, it would be good. If she was staring out of the window, then Serafina would have to try a little harder.

It turned out to be the second.

Steeling herself, Serafina went over to the Louis XVI couch. She couldn't help noticing that the fabric was threadbare in places and the gilt was chipped. The second that shabby chic fell out of favour they'd be in real trouble.

She greeted Francesca with a hug and kissed

both cheeks. 'Mamma. I bought you your favourites.' She handed over the flowers.

Francesca's eyes widened. 'But peonies are really expensive.'

'I bought them because I love you and I thought you'd like them.' Serafina damped down the disappointment. Maybe it wasn't possible to put a sparkle in her mother's eyes or bring her a moment of joy. But she couldn't stop trying, or she'd found herself sucked into the same quicksand of doom and gloom. At least *she* would enjoy the scent and colour of the flowers. 'Shall I put them in water for you?'

'Yes, do that.' Some of her disappointment must've shown in her face, because Francesca added, 'I'm sorry I snapped, *bella*. My hip aches today.'

It was an excuse, and both of them knew it. 'Have a rest, Mamma. I'll go and make dinner. Or I can order something in, if you like.'

Francesca sighed. 'This house. I *hate* this house. It's mouldering away. The only good thing about it is the view.'

At least her mother could see *one* good thing about the palazzo. Serafina held on to that. 'The house will be fine when we've fixed it up.'

'Will it? This house is unlucky. And we have no money to fix it up because your father gambled away everything we had. And we can't sell it because of the lawyers.' Francesca shook her head mournfully. 'I don't know what we're going to do.'

Serafina didn't dare tell her mother about the museum. It would send Francesca into total catastrophe mode. 'Leave it to me, Mamma. Try not to worry,' Serafina said. 'I'll make you some coffee and sort out dinner.'

And she really hoped that Gianni would help her find some real answers to her situation, next week.

CHAPTER THREE

GIANNI CHOSE THE high-speed direct train from Rome to Venice, to avoid changing trains and giving himself time to work without interruptions. But when the train stopped at Padova, half an hour from Venice, he found himself staring out of the window, thinking about Serafina.

Part of him thought this whole trip was insane. If she didn't have the money to do the work, what was the point of him even going to assess the house?

On the other hand, how could he resist the temptation to assess a centuries-old building that hadn't been touched within living memory? It was the kind of job he loved most—and that was why he'd fallen out with his father. Gianni's father had been keen on ultra-modern designs and loved concrete; whereas Gianni preferred more old-fashioned designs, and liked to see how modern materials could be used seamlessly with traditional ones. Their clashes had left Gianni frustrated that his dad refused to see his point of view or even consider a different way of doing things; it convinced him that his dad didn't respect him or think him good enough to take over from him when he was ready to retire.

And now he'd never get his dad's approval.

His dad definitely wouldn't have approved of this new job.

Though even considering this job had nothing to do with a secret rebellion or a yearning to prove himself. If he was honest, Serafina Ardizzone herself was the real lure to the Venetian project. In the short time he'd spent with her, he'd realised that she was bright, full of energy and sparkle, and it made him wonder why on earth Tom Burford had let her walk out of his life. Gianni had no intention of looking at the gossip pages and soaking up all the speculation; he'd seen a story saying that her engagement to the film star had ended a few months ago, and the reasons behind it were none of his business. But, if Serafina had been engaged to him, he knew he wouldn't have let her go so easily. He would've done his best to fix whatever the problem was.

Right now, beneath that sparkle, he had a feeling Serafina wasn't happy. Not just because she, like him, was grieving for a lost parent. There was something vulnerable about her. Was she shouldering the burden of the palazzo alone? What about her mum? Did she have any family or friends on her side, people who could advise her or be a sounding board? He was lucky in that his sister Flora was always there for him, and so was their mum; but did Serafina have anyone?

And why was he even letting himself think about Serafina in any terms other than that of client? Even if she was single, Gianni had no plans to get involved with anyone. He was busy with his job and repairing his family's reputation. He didn't have the time or the space in his life for a relationship—or the inclination, after the way Elena had broken their engagement mere days after there had been a suggestion of a problem in his business. Her family hadn't thought him good enough for her, and she hadn't loved him enough to disagree with them. He wasn't giving another posh woman the chance to use him and dump him; he'd rather put his energies into his business.

Yet he still couldn't concentrate on his paperwork.

And he knew it was because he'd be seeing Serafina.

Almost as if she knew he was thinking of her, and she was thinking of him too, his phone pinged with a text message and her name flashed up on the screen.

When you get off the train, walk down the steps at the entrance. I'll be waiting for you in front of the lamp-post. S

Gianni gave up all pretence of working after that; instead, he packed away his laptop and enjoyed the scenery. Crossing the causeway over the lagoon on a train felt distinctly odd; yet the views were stunning. He could see the city in the distance, the buildings packed close together and lit by the sun with a kind of haze round them. La Serenissima: The Most Serene, rising from the sea like a mirage. Venice really was otherworldly, like no place he'd ever visited before.

Once the train had come to a halt, he gathered his luggage together, headed for the entrance to the station and walked down the steps. In front of the station was a green lamp-post with three old-fashioned lanterns; and in front of the lamp-post was Serafina, leaning casually against it with one foot tucked behind the other, as if she was preparing to step forward.

She looked like a nineteen-fifties film star, wearing a brightly patterned fuchsia-pink scarf tied round her hair, navy capri pants, a navy-and-white-striped top, a white shirt with the sleeves rolled up to act as a light jacket, deck shoes to match her scarf, and a pair of designer sunglasses. And she was holding a placard that said 'Gianni Leto'. It was completely unnecessary, given that they'd already met and knew what each other looked like, but he couldn't help smiling. Being met like this made him feel as if he were special.

If he were one of her guests, he'd be thrilled to
bits by the welcome.

Should he kiss her on the cheek?

But, technically speaking, he was here as her
consultant rather than a friend. Plus, for all he
knew, his attraction to her was completely one-
sided. Feeling slightly wrong-footed, and determined to seem businesslike, he held out a hand
to shake hers. 'Good to see you again, Serafina.
Thank you for meeting me.'

'You're welcome, Gianni.' Her smile was bright
and made him feel warm from the inside out.
'How was your journey?'

'Good, thanks.'

Gianni discovered that the handshake was a
mistake. Just as last time, the feel of her skin
against his sent adrenalin prickling down his
spine, unsettling him. 'Are we taking the water
bus?' he asked, needing to distract himself from
his reaction to Serafina.

'It's your first time in Venice. No,' she said,
leading him away from the yellow sign for the
vaporetto stop and towards a pier. 'For your very
first trip in Venice, you need to travel by water
taxi. The *motoscafi* aren't allowed on the Grand
Canal during peak hours, apart from access, but
at least this way you'll get to see a bit more of the
city than you would on a *vaporetto*.' She smiled.
'I would've collected you and driven you myself,

but sadly our boat gave up the ghost a couple of years ago and it costs too much to repair. Though, if we had repaired it, I would've persuaded my father to convert it to an electric engine. They're much better for the people—and the buildings.'

She was conscious of the environment, then. That sat well with him.

'I'll show you the Grand Canal properly at some point during the week,' she said. 'And I assume, given what you do, that you'll want to see the famous buildings. I hope you don't mind being up early, because that for me is when the city's at her best.'

'It's fine by me,' he said. 'And yes, I'd love to see the buildings. The Palazzo Ducale in particular.'

'I guessed you might. I've got us timed tickets for tomorrow, to skip the queue,' she said.

The water taxi driver took Gianni's luggage and helped them both on board. Once the boat had gone under the pedestrian bridge by the train station, their driver turned off the Grand Canal onto a narrower, quieter waterway.

'I'm not even going to talk to you from now until we're back at the house,' Serafina said. 'Sit back and enjoy the view—and let Venice introduce herself to you. She's at her best in the little hidden corners.'

Gianni felt like a celebrity, travelling down the

turquoise waters of the canal in a private boat. Every so often, the sunlight caught the water and made it sparkle; and all around him were tall buildings with narrow windows, beautiful doorways and metal grilles. When a bridge—a mixture of stone, brick, wood and iron—crossed the canal, underneath every single one he could see silvery reflections from the water rippling across the stone.

Even though the builder in him winced inwardly at the damage the water had done to the structure of the buildings, at the same he couldn't help being enchanted by the chipped and faded stucco, and the timeless elegance of the architecture. How many people had passed this way over the years, nurturing secret hopes and dreams and falling under the spell of the city?

He heard a nearby church clock strike the quarter-hour, and then another and another, echoing away into the distance: and then it struck him how quiet it was here. No cars, no furious horn-beeping or engines revving or screech of tyres as someone braked. This was another world.

The driver expertly took them through the maze of canals, and then they were back on the Grand Canal itself and Gianni realised they must be near to the palazzo. When the boat pulled up by a narrow pontoon that was clearly a private entrance, he recognised Ca' d'Ardizzone from the photographs Serafina had sent him. Close up, he could see the damage to the stucco on the front of the palazzo and the unevenness of the colour.

What would it be like inside? Had her photographs shown the damage as it truly was, or minimised it?

The driver helped them both out of the boat, sketched a salute to Serafina, and drove off.

'Welcome to Ca' d'Ardizzone, Gianni,' she said.

'Thank you.' He inclined his head. 'How much do I owe you for the water taxi?'

'Nothing. It's my pleasure.'

Pleasure.

Why did that word suddenly make him feel hot all over?

This was ridiculous. He was here on business. Well, *mainly* business. Which meant he needed to get himself back into professional mode instead of mooning over her. 'Thank you,' he said again.

She opened the door and ushered him in.

'Centuries ago, my family imported wines and spices,' she said. 'There's a second water gate on the side of the palazzo, and that's the one the merchants would have used. But this one—though we don't tend to use it much nowadays—would have been for guests.'

The entrance hall was enormous, running from the front to the back of the building; it clearly fol-

lowed the classical floor plan of a Venetian palazzo, with a *portego*, or large entrance hall, having
all the rooms leading off it. The floor was Venetian terrazzo, crushed marble set in lime and
then ground and polished to a shine; the plain
wooden ceilings were high; and there was a grand
staircase with marble newel posts and delicate
wrought-iron balustrades leading up to the next
floor.

It was stunning.

'And this is the area you're planning to rent to
a museum?' he asked.

'Yes. It's perfect for exhibitions. Look at the
light,' she said.

He had to agree. Superficially, the room was
perfect. Close up, the imperfections would show
and reveal the damage—he could definitely smell
damp, and he suspected there was crumbling
plaster behind that wall-covering—but he could
see the potential.

'I'll give you a super-quick tour before lunch,
but let me show you to your room first, so you
can freshen up. I'm afraid we don't have en-suite
bathrooms,' she added apologetically, 'but there
is a bathroom next door to your room.'

'That sounds good. I'll follow you up,' he said.

Portraits in gold frames hung on the wall next
to the staircase, following the line of the stairs upwards. Her ancestors, he presumed. All of them

looked stern and gave off a faint air of disapproval, or maybe that was simply the way they'd been posed.

At the top of stairs was another enormous hall.

'The kitchen's through there,' she said, indicating the first room, 'and I'm going to sort out some coffee.' She waved her hand towards the side of the house facing the canal. 'Ballroom, dining room, drawing room, sitting room, library. The bedrooms are all at the back of the house, mainly because it's a bit less humid there. The kitchen's at the back, too.' She led him past several doorways. 'This is your room. I hope you'll find it comfortable, but let me know if there's anything you need.' She smiled. 'There are fresh towels on the bed. Come and find me in the kitchen when you're ready.'

The room was a good size, with parquet flooring and a thick rug in shades of red, blue and gold. The wide bed had a gilt and dark blue velvet headboard, the Louis XVI settee was also gilt and dark blue velvet, and there was a mirror with an ornate gilt frame above the gilt and cream dressing table. A matching ottoman with a blue-velvet-upholstered top stood next to the dressing table and the cream and gilt wardrobe. The wallpaper was faded in places, and by the window was an area of water-staining. In winter, Gianni thought, this room would smell as damp as the downstairs hall had. On closer inspection, the upholstery was faded and slightly threadbare in places, and the gilt and paint were definitely distressed—albeit from age, rather than a designer's judicious sand-papering. Shabby chic, as Serafina had called it. Designers would pay a fortune for that effect; but Gianni could imagine how the room must have looked when everything was still new. Opulent and comfortable at the same time.

He took one of the towels from the bed and went to explore the bathroom. A quick inspection showed him terrazzo flooring, some tiling on the walls that had cracked in places and at the very least needed new grouting and sealant, and it looked as if the brass taps were at least a century old. When he tried the cold water tap, it worked without a problem. Perhaps the plumbing had been put in order relatively recently; though, in a house that was more than five hundred years old, 'recently' could mean any time in the last fifty years. He wondered if the electric wiring had even been looked at since it was first installed. From the colour of the socket next to the bed, he had a feeling it hadn't.

When she'd first said that the house would breach all health and safety conditions, he'd thought she might be exaggerating. But now he was pretty sure she'd been stating the truth.

He splashed his face, dried it, and went to find Serafina in the kitchen.

The room was a strange mixture of ancient and new: a terrazzo floor, several vintage dressers and shelving, an antique marble-topped table and chairs at the far end of the room, and then a very modern fridge, cooker and washing machine.

'Perfect timing,' she said, holding a mug of coffee aloft. 'Do you take milk or sugar?'

'No milk and half a sugar, please,' he said.

She finished preparing his drink and handed it to him. 'Mamma and I tend to eat in here, rather than in the dining room, if there are fewer than six of us. Or on the terrace, if the weather's nice. Come and have the super-quick guided tour. Bring your coffee.'

He sipped it gratefully—relieved to find that the coffee was good and he wasn't going to have to be polite about it—and followed her back into the hall.

'This is the ballroom. Apparently my great-grandparents were fond of parties and used it quite a lot, though I can't remember the last time a party was held here. Probably when I was very small.'

The floor was parquet in here, rather than terrazzo; Gianni assumed that the dust sheets were draping over sofas and small tables, which were probably in the same shabby condition as the furniture in his bedroom. The furniture was all set against the walls; he'd need to move it to check the condition of the walls behind it. Mirrors reflected the light from the huge windows and were strategically placed to catch the light from the glass chandeliers, making the room feel beautifully spacious and airy. Large glass doors led to the balcony; he could imagine the room being full of people dancing, drinking champagne and chattering, then going onto the balcony for a breath of fresh air.

'The dining room,' Serafina said at the next door. 'Though, as I said earlier, we don't use it that often.'

Again, the furniture was dust-sheeted: what he assumed was a very large table and chairs sat in the middle, with console tables and cabinets at the sides. There were plenty of pictures in gilt frames on the walls, and he wondered why she hadn't sold some of them to pay for the building work. Or maybe they, like the palazzo itself, were entailed and couldn't be sold.

'Drawing room. Which we don't use,' she said. 'I'm afraid the dust-sheeting is a bit ugly, but it saves a lot of cleaning.'

It must be hard, he thought, showing someone round your home—a place where your family had lived for centuries—and knowing that person was about to find every single fault with it, even if you'd actually asked them to do an honest assessment. And every fault would cost money and time to fix. It would be daunting even if you were used to building work; and he could see that she was trying to hide her worries behind that over-bright voice. Part of him wanted to give her a hug and tell her that it would be all right; but, apart from the fact that it wouldn't be appropriate to hug her, he didn't believe in giving false promises.

The next room was the sitting room. 'Now, we *do* use this,' she said. 'It would be a crime to waste the view.'

Again there were large glass doors which led to a balcony; he went over to admire the view of the Grand Canal. 'You're right. It's fabulous,' he said.

The sofas here were made comfortable with cushions and throws, which he suspected covered up threadbare materials; there was also a flat-screen television and an ancient-looking piano. 'Do you play?' he asked.

'A little,' she said.

Which could mean anything from picking out a tune very haltingly with one finger through to being concert pianist standard. He didn't know Serafina well enough yet to know if she was over-modest or straightforward.

'The library,' she said, taking him to the next room. 'It used to be my father's den. Now it's my workspace.'

The desk overlooked the canal and was perfectly clear except for a laptop; the walls were lined with bookshelves; and there were a couple of large leather armchairs that looked very uncomfortable. He couldn't imagine her curled up in one, lost in a book.

Once they were back in the main hall, she gestured to the side of the house that didn't overlook the canal. 'Six bedrooms and three bathrooms, all pretty much like the ones you're using. The next floor up has a similar layout, but all the furniture's dust-sheeted, to save cleaning,' she said. 'It's where my grandparents used to live. They had bedrooms at opposite ends of the floor, and separate sitting rooms and dining rooms.'

Which sounded as if they were either hugely old-fashioned or loathed each other. Or was that the way the upper classes lived? 'Do you remember that?' he asked.

'Not really. They died about twenty-five years ago, when I was still very young,' Serafina said. 'My father didn't speak much about them. Mamma doesn't say much, either.'

Which reminded him of his earlier concern. 'Does your mother mind me staying here?'

She smiled. 'Mamma's staying with her sister this week.'

Which didn't answer his question, and it made him wonder: did her mother even know he was here? And, if not, why had Serafina kept his visit from her? Was it anything like the way Elena had kept their relationship a secret from her family, at first? But he couldn't think how to ask without it sounding belligerent. He wanted to work with her, not fight with her.

'The top floor is more of the same,' she said. 'Originally they were the servants' rooms. They've been shut off or used as store rooms for as long as I can remember.' She shrugged. 'And now I'm the custodian of the palazzo. I don't want to let it moulder away. I want it to be used. To *shine*.'

Exactly how he'd feel about the place, in her shoes. He could see past the shabbiness to the bones of the house, and they were beautiful. The proportions were perfect. 'I get that,' he said. 'But you need to do this with your eyes open. There isn't a quick, cheap fix.' He looked her in the eyes. 'Well, there is: you can paper over the cracks. But if you don't solve the underlying problems they'll just get worse—and it'll cost more in the long run.'

'Cost.' Her face went tight for a moment. Then she glanced at her watch. 'Shall we have some lunch?'

Clearly she needed some time to come to terms with reality. He wouldn't push her too hard, too fast. He had a whole week to help her face reality. 'That would be great. What can I do to help?'

'Go and sit on the balcony, and enjoy the view,' she directed. 'Would you like some wine?'

'Water's fine, thanks,' he said. He wanted to work with a clear head.

'The doors in the sitting room open out onto the balcony. I'll bring everything through. It's going to be very simple, I'm afraid, but I'll take you to an *osteria* on the other side of the canal for dinner tonight, so you get to experience proper Venetian food.' There was a hint of mischief in her eyes as she added, 'Unless you insist on eating at a place with Michelin stars, though I can't guarantee they'll offer you lobster.'

He couldn't help smiling back, remembering that conversation and how he'd tried to push her. 'Proper Venetian food sounds good.'

The balcony ran across the whole front of the house; there were terracotta pots squeezed in between the balusters, filled with herbs and geraniums. At one side there was a metal bistro table with a glass top, and four chairs; she'd already placed cushions on the seats and set the table with cutlery, crockery, glasses and linen napkins. And the view was unparalleled: the turquoise waters of the Grand Canal, lined with palazzos and churches. Rather than sitting down, he leaned his forearms on the balcony and looked out. Everywhere he looked, there were domes and interesting windows and architectural details. He could quite see why Venice turned so many people's heads. The city was beautiful.

Like Serafina. Which was exhilarating and terrifying at the same time. She was the first woman who'd made him feel this pull of attraction since Elena: which meant that maybe at long last he was putting all the heartbreak behind him. On the other hand, Elena's family hadn't thought he was good enough for them, and they weren't even proper aristocrats—unlike Serafina. A titled woman's family would no doubt look down even further on him.

He was going to have to put a lid on his attraction to her and keep things strictly professional.

Having a stranger in her house was harder than Serafina had expected.

OK, this week had been her idea, and she'd thought it was a good one at the time. But she'd forgotten how gorgeous Gianni Leto was. How the touch of his palm against hers made her skin tingle and made her catch her breath. How beautiful his mouth was.

She couldn't afford to let herself fall for him. Even though the sensible side of her knew that the family curse was a ridiculous superstition, if she looked back at her love-life she'd fallen for one Mr Wrong after another. Men who hadn't felt as deeply for her as she'd felt about them. And then, there had been Mr Completely Disastrously Wrong: Tom Burford, the movie star who'd swept her off her feet and made her believe that he'd really loved her for herself. Except he'd been acting, because he'd wanted her aristocratic connections rather than her. He'd carried on having flings with whoever took his fancy, and she'd only found out because she'd flown out on a surprise visit and found him in bed with someone else.

It had been the final disillusionment that had stopped her believing in love.

Falling for Gianni Leto would be a huge mistake. She needed him to fall in love with the palazzo and with Venice, yet at the same time she had to keep her heart intact. She'd be bright and charming, the way she'd always been at work, pointing out all the positives and dealing quietly with the negatives. And she'd definitely have to ignore the way her blood felt as if it fizzed through her veins whenever Gianni smiled at her.

Focus, she told herself. She sliced the bread, put it in a wicker basket and put the basket on a tray, along with a platter of cheese and a dish of sliced tomatoes sprinkled with fresh basil. She added a jug of iced water with slices of lime, then carried the lot out to the balcony.

He was standing with his arms resting on the stone, looking out to the canal, and she itched to sketch him. Which was strange, because her pen-

and-ink drawings and watercolours were all land-scapes, slices of canal and buildings or a close-up of a detail that interested her. She didn't usually bother sketching people. Why him? What was so different about him?

It wasn't a question she'd let herself dwell on. The answer was potentially way too distracting. Instead, she took a deep breath and set the tray down on the table.

He turned to face her, and that smile made her heart feel as if it had done a backflip. 'This is a lovely spot.'

'It's good for eating, or reading, or just watching the world go by.' And sketching, when she had time. Not that he needed to know about that. It wasn't relevant. 'Please help yourself. The bread's from the bakery round the corner, and they're very good.'

'Thank you.' He waited until she'd sat down before taking his seat. Old-fashioned manners: she liked that.

'Right,' she said brightly. 'About this week. Obviously you need time to assess the palazzo; but I thought during the week I could show you some of the famous buildings in the city, and maybe some of the less famous ones. There isn't any ballet or opera on this week, but there are plenty of string quartet concerts. I could get tickets for one evening, if you'd like to go.'

'That's kind of you to offer,' he said, 'but classical music's not my sort of thing.'

Which meant he wouldn't be enthused about her idea of holding small concerts of classical Venetian music in her ballroom, then. 'Sorry. Most of the music venues tend to be classical,' she said, 'or jazz. But there are plenty of other things we can do. And I'd like to take you to see one palazzo that's been restored, so you can see for yourself what this house might have looked like in its heyday.'

'Do you have any old photographs?' he asked. 'Something that might show the interiors?'

'There are probably some in the old albums.' She bit her lip. 'Sorry, I should've thought to look through them earlier.'

'No problem.' He looked at her. 'I'm guessing you've been thrown into this in the deep end.'

'Not *exactly*. I'm part of a long line of people who didn't pay enough attention to what was happening right under their noses, I'm afraid. I kind of got what I deserve. Particularly as an art historian—I should've known better,' she said. 'Though I admit I'm a bit worried about the assessment and how bad the damage actually is. And how long it will take to fix.' She knew she'd have to tell him about the time constraints, and probably sooner rather than later, but she didn't want him to take a negative view of the situation before he'd even started. She wanted to start with

what the damage was, how long it would take—
and then, if necessary, tackle how it could be sped
up in time to rehouse the museum. 'Is there anything I can do to help? Hold one end of a tape
measure for you or something?'

Gianni didn't have the heart to tell her that he normally used a laser measure, particularly as she'd
been honest with him about the fact her family
hadn't paid enough attention to the house over the
years. 'I'm happy for you to be alongside me as I
work. I can show you what I'm looking at as we
go, and you can ask questions about anything that
isn't clear. I believe in transparency for my clients;
and you in turn can tell me everything you know
about the palazzo. That way we're both working
with the best information possible.'

'Thank you,' she said. 'I'll try not to get under
your feet or start micromanaging, though you
might need to tell me to shut up.'

He couldn't help laughing. 'I wish all my clients took that attitude. And, by the way, this bread
is excellent.'

'You're welcome.'

She smiled at him, a genuine smile rather than
the professional one he suspected she'd been using
with him so far, and his pulse sped up. When she
smiled like that, it made him feel as if the sun had
just come out after a long, dull, rainy day. And
he wanted more of that feeling.

After lunch, he insisted on helping her wash up. Then he collected his damp meter, laser measure, clipboard and camera from his room.

'No computer?' she asked when he joined her back in the kitchen.

'Not at this stage. I think better with a pen than with a keyboard—it's something to do with the connection between the hand and the brain,' he said, 'and photographs help.'

'It's the same for me at the museum,' she said.

'What does an art historian do?' he asked. 'Do you write about art?'

'Sometimes. The museum where I work specialises in women's art, and I organise exhibitions and write the catalogue and the notes that go with the exhibits. Sometimes I give a talk or do the occasional guided tour, and as a board member I persuade people to give us grants or lend us beautiful things.'

That was where her professional smile came from, then. Was she going to try to persuade him into something, the way she persuaded people at work?

Then again, she already had. He'd agreed to do the assessment in exchange for a week's break at the palazzo, with her as his tour guide.

'Let's start with the ground floor and work upwards,' he said.

He walked round the ground floor and sketched the floor plan first, marking in doors and windows as he went, then went back to each room in turn to measure the dimensions.

'I feel very stupid,' she said, 'not thinking that you'd have a laser measure.'

For a second, he thought he could see the sheen of tears in her eyes. Had someone made her feel stupid, in the past? Or was she just worried sick about exactly how much work the palazzo needed—and how she was going to finance that?

Weirdly, he found himself wanting to protect her. Which was crazy. Apart from the fact that he'd already worked out she was very capable, he couldn't snap his fingers and make all the problems vanish.

But maybe working with him would help to distract her from her worries, just for a little while. For long enough to get her equilibrium back. He could at least do that for her. 'A metal ruler has its place,' he said. 'But a laser measure's accurate. And, short of us having to use a ladder, it's the easiest way to measure the height of the walls as well.' He marked the measurements on his floor plan as he made them. 'You know you asked if you can help? I'm going to take a few moisture readings, and it'd be great if you could write them down for me.' Wanting to put her at her ease, he smiled at her. 'You can be in charge of the clipboard.'

'That sounds good.'

He sketched out a plan of the wall and labelled the points where he planned to measure. 'I'll call them out in order, if you wouldn't mind writing next to the labels?'

His fingers accidentally brushed hers when he handed her the pen and the clipboard, and again that zing of awareness went down his spine. So much for trying to distract her; it felt more as if *she* was distracting *him*.

Gianni's touch sent adrenalin fizzing through Serafina's veins, which was ridiculous. For a second, her thoughts were scattered; and then she realised he was waiting for a response to his question.

'Sure. Next to the labels. Got it.'

'I'm hoping that an art historian's handwriting isn't like a medic's.'

His words defused the tension, to her relief. 'No. Mine's legible.'

'Good.'

He was methodical about where he took the measurements, and she wrote down the numbers he called out. 'Are they good or bad?' she asked when he finished.

'Mixed,' he said. 'I need to take some photographs before we do the next room.'

His voice was neutral and she couldn't tell anything from his expression. 'That sounds faintly ominous.'

'It's practical,' he said. 'I've been looking at how other buildings in the city deal with *acqua alta*. There's one in particular I want to visit, because they let the water come in through a metal gate and channel it out.' He smiled at her. 'It's a museum now. Hopefully you'll know someone there who will allow me to poke about and ask questions.'

She relaxed again. 'I probably do. Or we'll know people in common, at least. It should be fine.'

'Does this level flood?'

'Not really,' she said. 'We're a bit higher up here than in St Mark's. I know they had terrible floods when my dad was a child and he told me he could remember it being flooded up to the third step, but there's been nothing like since then.'

'That's useful. Thank you.' He took the clipboard back from her, and made a note.

But the photographs were worrying. Particularly when he looked at the surfaces behind the wall-coverings that had peeled away. Was her palazzo rotting from the ground up? Could it be saved at all? Was he going to tell her that this was all a waste of time?

Once they'd finished the ground floor, they headed up the stairs.

'These are all your great-whatever-grandfathers?' he asked, indicating the portraits.

'Yes. There's one of my father and my grandfather in my office. They're in date order, the newest portraits at the bottom—though you probably already guessed that from the way they're dressed.'

'None of them are smiling,' he said. 'Or is that a convention in art?'

'Partly convention, because a portrait was formal and smiling was a breach of etiquette—back in the eighteenth century it meant you were poor, drunk, or lewd,' she explained. 'But mostly it was practical. If you sit for a portrait, you have to hold the same position for hours. And it's impossible to maintain a smile for that long. You end up with pretty much a rictus grin, and that would detract from whatever the person commissioning the portrait wanted to get across—whether that was power, wealth, learning or virtue. You might get a bit of a smirk, like Mona Lisa's, but that's about it.'

'I had no idea,' he said.

'But you have a point. They don't look happy.' She thought again of the family curse. Despite her aunt's explanation for her parents and her grandparents, there had been a whole line of unhappy Ardizzones and it showed in every single portrait. The only one who had looked even slightly happy was Marianna, in her miniature: and Marianna had had the saddest ending.

They went through the rooms in the *piano nob-*

ile with the same thoroughness; it took time, because Gianni needed to move the furniture to check the walls behind them. 'I'd be happier if I could move the pictures as well, to see what's behind them.'

'I had to do that to inventory them for inheritance tax purposes,' she said. 'There isn't any mould or any sign of peeling wallpaper.'

Unlike by the windows; the worst of it was hidden by floor-length drapes, but she knew there were problems. And the expression on his face when he'd checked the window frames told her that they'd need at the very least repairing, if not full replacement.

'Are you sure your mother won't mind me assessing her room?' Gianni asked, stopping by the doorway.

'My mother...' Serafina winced. 'Let's just say she worries. If she knew you were a guest, she'd make you very welcome.' Or as welcome as she could; they'd had so few visitors over the last few years, apart from Vittoria, that Francesca was out of practice. 'If she had any idea you were assessing the house, she'd panic. I want to spare her all the worrying, so I haven't told her, and that's why she's staying with Aunt Vittoria this week. But if she did know about the assessment, then of course she'd understand why you need to see her room and she'd be fine about it.'

* * *

Serafina was clearly very protective of her mother and had taken the kind way out. Gianni liked that—and he was also relieved that it wasn't because she was ashamed of the stuff that was going on between them under the surface, the way he'd eventually realised Elena had been. Though he still felt faintly uncomfortable about invading Contessa Francesca's private space.

'I'll make us some more coffee,' Serafina said, when they got to her own room.

Yeah. Assessing her private space, in front of her, would've felt very odd. Gianni compartmentalised his thoughts, switched into professional mode, and did the measuring and checking.

When he'd finished, he went to join her in the kitchen.

'Let's have a break before the next floor,' she suggested. 'Shall we go and sit on the balcony again?'

'That'd be nice.'

She put some ring-shaped cookies on a plate, and ushered him out to the balcony. 'Help yourself,' she said, indicating the cookies.

He took one. Buttery and lemony, rich and tart at the same time. He could easily scoff the lot. 'These are amazing,' he said. 'I assume they're from the same bakery as the bread?'

'No. I made them this morning from my best

friend's *nonna*'s recipe.' She smiled at him. 'I was thinking what you said about the portraits. I do have one with a slight smile, as it happens. And, because I'm a terrible nerd when it comes to art, I'd rather like to show it to you. Excuse me a moment.' She disappeared back into the sitting room, and returned with a box, which contained something wrapped in paper. 'Acid-free paper, for protection,' she explained, and unwrapped the artwork before handing it to him.

It was a miniature of a woman in a rose-coloured silk dress, her fair hair in an updo. The woman was smiling; it wasn't a broad smile, like you'd see in modern photographs, but the smile definitely reached her eyes.

'This is my Great-however-many-times-Aunt Marianna,' Serafina said. 'I think it's actually my favourite piece of art in the palazzo. The style owes a lot to Rosalba Carriera, though sadly it isn't one of hers.'

'I assume Rosalba Carriera is a famous painter, but I'm afraid I've never heard of her,' Gianni admitted.

'She was an eighteenth-century Venetian painter. I studied her as part of my Master's course,' Serafina said. 'We have some of her work at the museum.'

There was one thing he didn't understand. 'If you love this painting, why keep it wrapped up and out of sight? Why not keep it on show?'

'Because this is a watercolour, and watercolours fade easily. It's why you'll often see miniatures displayed in a case covered with a curtain in a museum, to protect them from the light but still give people access to them,' she said. 'Carriera started out decorating snuff boxes, then moved over to painting miniatures. At the time, miniatures were painted on vellum, but she experimented and found that ivory worked better. Her portraits are beautiful. She used white chalk over her pastels, to make things more luminous.'

Right then, Gianni thought, Serafina looked luminous; talking about art made her light up. And that brightness made the whole room feel as if it had lit up. He wanted to get to know this woman better. A lot better. And he was starting to see a connection between them in their shared love of architecture—his in general, and hers for the palazzo.

She took her phone from the pocket of her capri pants and brought up some images. 'Look at these. They're gorgeous.' She smiled ruefully. 'Though I'd better shut up. I can drone on for hours about Rosalba Carriera.'

Gianni thought that he could listen to Serafina talk for hours. She had a beautiful voice. If she were reading the dullest list of statistics, she'd still manage to hold his attention completely. She'd said that she sometimes gave lectures; he'd bet that everyone was spellbound by her.

'You look like your great-aunt, though obviously your hair's much darker,' he said, handing the portrait back.

'Her hair was probably the same colour as mine, underneath the powder. It was the fashion to powder your hair, back then,' Serafina said. 'Sadly, she didn't have a happy ending. She fell in love with a local man, and her parents forbade her to see him because they wanted her to marry someone else. She planned to elope with him, but while she was trying to creep out of the house she tripped on the stairs, fell down them and broke her neck.'

'That's really sad,' Gianni said.

'Isn't it?' Serafina wrapped up the miniature again.

'What made you become an art historian?' he asked, wanting to know what drove her.

'Wherever you go in Venice, you see art,' she said. 'When I was small, I wanted to know more about the pictures and the statues. Who made them, how they lived, why they chose those particular themes. Especially when I learned that a painting is more than a pretty picture of someone; the way they're posed, the way they're dressed and the items in the painting tell you more about that person. If there's a Renaissance portrait of a woman and she's wearing pearls, the person commissioning that portrait wants you to know she's pure and chaste, because that's what pearls symbolise, and also very rich, because pearls were rare and very expensive. Marianna's wearing rubies in her portrait—a choker, earrings, a brooch on her bodice and two smaller ones on her shoulders. Rubies are associated with purity, wealth, wisdom and calming wrath. Assuming her father was the one who had the miniature painted, any potential husband would take one look at it and know exactly what her character was like.'

He wouldn't have had a clue, and he loved the fact that Serafina could fill in all the details for him but without making him feel as if she were lecturing or as if he were stupid. 'Does your family still own the rubies?'

Serafina shook her head. 'Apparently they went missing after she died. They're probably somewhere at the bottom of the canal, buried under a great deal of mud; or maybe someone melted down the jewellery and reset the stones. Nobody knows.'

'There are a lot of paintings in the palazzo,' he said. 'Have you thought about—?' He stopped, realising how rude and intrusive the question was.

'Selling them to finance the house repairs?' she asked.

'Yes. Though I assume they're entailed, like the house,' he said.

'They're not, but unfortunately the ones that

would have raised a lot of money are copies. The rest are portraits of my family, painted by artists who followed a trend rather than set one. The amount they'd raise at auction, after tax, wouldn't make up for the effort of trying to sell them.' She shrugged, as if to say that it was a pity but she'd have to live with the situation. 'I'll just put Marianna away safely.'

'Sure. And we can get started on the next floor.' He drained his coffee. 'I'll wash up.'

'You're a guest. You don't need to wash up.'

'I'm not quite a guest. I'm here to assess the palazzo,' he corrected. 'And it won't kill me to wash up some cups.'

'Then thank you,' she said. 'I'll see you in the kitchen.'

By the time they were halfway through the rooms on next floor—rooms that clearly hadn't been used for a long while, and smelled musty— they were both covered in dust. Gianni just about managed to resist the urge to wipe a smudge off Serafina's cheek.

She glanced at her watch. 'I guess it's a bit naive of me. I didn't think the assessment would take this long.'

'It does if you do it properly,' he said.

'I've got a table booked at one of my favourite places, and I had kind of planned for us to go out at six, to show you a bit of the area,' she said.

'We can do that,' he said. 'Let's stop now and continue later.'

'Wonderful,' she said. 'Though I think we could both do with a shower before we go out.' There was distinct colour in her face when she added, 'The plumbing can be a bit temperamental and doesn't always like it if more than one shower runs at a time. I'll let you shower first.'

Gianni had a moment when he imagined them sharing a shower, and it made him feel hot all over. Desire licked down his spine as he imagined her with wet hair slicked back, laughing up at him. How soft her skin would feel as he lathered it and then, as the water washed the suds away, how her eyes would darken with need, and she'd reach up to...

Oh, for pity's sake. Since when he did start fantasising about a woman he hardly knew—a potential client, too? 'Thanks,' he muttered. To stop himself adding something completely inappropriate, he made himself think about damp proofing methods.

She glanced at her watch. 'I was thinking we could have an aperitif and *cichéti*, then take a stroll around San Polo before dinner. Is that OK with you?'

'Cichéti?' he asked.

'Little snacks to go with your drink,' she said. 'The Venetian version of *mezze*, or perhaps tapas, but don't ever say that to a bar owner.'

'Noted,' he said, smiling back. 'What's the dress code?'

'Smart casual,' she said. 'See you on the balcony when you're ready?'

'OK. I'll knock on your door when I've finished in the shower, so you're not hanging around waiting for me.'

'That's kind, but actually I'll be in the drawing room, seeing if I can find those photos you asked about,' she said. 'Can you come and give me a yell there?'

'Sure.'

She smiled her thanks at him, and again Gianni had that weird sensation as if his heart was doing a somersault. It unsettled him to the point where, once he'd scrubbed the dust from his skin and his hair, he switched the shower to cold to put some common sense back in his head.

This week was meant to be about work. He shouldn't let himself blur the boundaries—no matter how attractive he found Serafina Ardizzone.

CHAPTER FOUR

WHILE GIANNI WAS SHOWERING, Serafina went into the drawing room and checked the cupboard where all the photographs were kept. She fished out the earliest albums; hopefully there would be something in there showing the interiors of the palazzo.

For exterior views, she knew of a couple of paintings that included Ca' d'Ardizzone. If she was very lucky, there might also be something in Ruskin's early daguerreotypes of Venice; or perhaps there would be some old photographs in an internet archive somewhere. Still sitting on the floor, she flicked into her phone and did a quick search. The first two archives had nothing, but she found a whole series of colour photographs from the end of the nineteenth century, which she bookmarked to check later.

There was a rap on the door, and she looked up.

'Shower's all yours,' he said.

Gianni was fully dressed, in a casual shirt and

chinos, but his hair was still damp and mussed from being towelled; and he looked so incredibly sexy that Serafina's pulse kicked up a notch.

'How did you get on with the photographs?' he asked.

'I've found our earliest family albums, but because I was checking for images on external archives I haven't started looking through them,' she said. 'Maybe we can do that together later.'

'Sounds good,' he said.

'See you in twenty minutes. Help yourself to coffee or something cold. Everything's in a sensible place in the kitchen,' she said, and left the albums on the table in the sitting room before heading for her own bathroom.

She showered swiftly, wrapped her hair in a towel while she changed into a pretty summer dress and added the lightest touch of make-up— mascara and lipstick—then plaited her still-damp hair to keep it out of the way. She added canvas shoes that were easy to walk in, and she was ready.

Gianni was sitting on the balcony, finishing a coffee and looking out at the view. His smile made her heart feel as if she'd done a backflip.

'How do you ever get anything done, living here?' he asked. 'I'd spend all my time looking at the view.'

'When I'm working from home, I use a timer,

otherwise I'd do exactly that,' she said with a rueful smile. 'Let's go and grab something to eat.'

She wouldn't let him wash up his mug before they left the palazzo, simply locking up after them and ushering him out towards the Rialto bridge.

'You can see why people photograph it so much,' he said. 'It's beautiful. The proportions are perfect.'

She smiled. 'I knew you'd like it.'

'And this leads to the market?'

'Yes. I was planning to take you there early on Wednesday morning, when you can see it at its best.'

'Look at this,' he marvelled as they walked up the steps. 'You can actually see where people's hands have brushed against the bridge and polished it over the years.'

At that moment, his hand brushed against hers. And she had to fight against the instinct to let her fingers tangle with his. This wasn't a date. She wanted Gianni to fall in love with the palazzo and the city, not with her. Because love for a place was permanent and reliable, whereas falling in love with a person wasn't. She'd fallen for Tom the moment she'd met him at a glitzy party held at the museum where she worked, and clearly she'd confused the man with the characters he'd played on screen: they were noble and brave and unselfish, whereas Tom had turned out to be a liar and a selfish cheat. He'd made her feel loved and cherished, but it had all been an act. When she'd walked into his flat and discovered her fiancé mid-shag with an actress who'd hoped to get a part in his next movie, it had broken her faith in her judgement. How could she have fallen for someone who'd use his position to prey on others? For a man who let his libido rule everything? For a man who'd professed to love her and hadn't meant a single word?

OK, so Gianni didn't seem like that. But how could she trust herself to see him clearly, when her judgement in men was so bad?

So instead, she made herself tell Gianni stories about the bridge and the area, pointing out the church where her favourite painting in the city was, before leading him through an alleyway.

'I promised you real Venice,' she said. 'Would you prefer an Aperol spritz or wine?'

'I'll have whatever you're having,' he said.

She smiled, and swiftly ordered a plate of snacks to share and two glasses of dry white wine. 'It's an *ombra*,' she explained when the wine arrived.

'A shadow?' He looked mystified.

'Centuries ago, the wine seller in St Mark's Square used to move his cart around to keep his wine in the shadow of the bell tower. Or so the story goes; gradually "meeting in the shadow of the bell tower" started to mean meeting someone for a glass of wine. Over the years, that got shortened to "shadow", meaning the wine itself, or a spritz.' She raised her glass. *'Salute.'*

He chinked his glass against hers. *'Salute.'*

His eyes were really beautiful. Dark and soulful. Serafina found herself leaning slightly towards him, and it made her panic: she hadn't reacted to anyone like this before, not even Tom. She couldn't risk falling for this man the way she'd fallen for Tom, only to be let down again. How could she be sure that his integrity in his business life would be matched in his private life? To distract herself from how attractive she found him, she told Gianni about the food. 'I've ordered things you're unlikely to find outside Venice. This is *sarde in saor,* sardines in a sweet and sour sauce. It was originally invented for sailors, as a way of preserving fish for long journeys and also adding a bit of vitamin C through the onions to prevent scurvy—and obviously the spices in the sauce are a nod to the city's trading history.'

'Are you sure you studied history of art and not social history?' he asked.

'I was born in Venice. You grow up with the stories,' she said, but inwardly she was pleased by the compliment. 'And *baccalà mantecato:* creamed dried cod, whipped into a mousse and served on grilled polenta.' She smiled. 'And fried stuffed zucchini flowers, which I know you have in Rome, but I happen to like them. Plus white asparagus wrapped in pancetta, and a slightly different bruschetta.'

She had the tourist patter off to a fine art, Gianni thought. And he loved the way she lit up when she spoke about her city and its customs. 'This all looks great,' he said.

'It tastes even better than it looks,' she said.

Which made him think of her mouth and wonder how it would taste...

He wasn't looking for a relationship. But flirting—something that he could stop before it went too far—might be fun.

'If you close your eyes,' he said, 'it heightens your other senses. How about I do that, and you test me on what I can actually taste?'

There was a tiny flush on her cheeks, and he guessed that she was thinking the same thing. Closed eyes. Tasting. *Kissing.*

Would she back away? Or would she flirt back?

Eventually she nodded. '*Sarde* first.'

He closed his eyes and concentrated on the flavour. 'The fish is good. The sauce: I can taste the sweetness of honey—' as sweet as he thought her mouth might be '—and sultanas and the sourness of vinegar. Pine nuts. Coriander?' He opened his eyes and kept his gaze fixed on hers.

'The only thing you missed was cloves,' she said. 'You're a foodie?'

'Sometimes. I'm guilty of not noticing what I eat, when I'm working,' he admitted. 'A sandwich is—well, just a sandwich.'

'Not in Venice, it isn't.' She smiled. 'I'll introduce you to *tramezzini* tomorrow.' She ate her share of the sardines. 'Which one do you want to try next?'

He picked the cod, which turned out to be garlicky and much nicer than he'd expected.

The bar was growing more crowded, and they had to stand closer together. By the time they'd reached the last of their *cichéti*, he'd ended up with a protective arm around her, and he was very aware of the warmth of her body against his.

'Last one,' she said.

'Bread, tomato and pesto—but there's something different. I can't work out what.' He opened his eyes. 'Tell me.'

'Nettles,' she said.

'Seriously?'

'Seriously.'

'Venice is full of surprises,' he said. One of them being her.

'There's still so much to see,' she said, and he had a feeling she wasn't only talking about her city.

'It's getting busy in here.' She glanced at her

watch. 'Our table will be ready in half an hour. Let me show you round San Polo.'

Gianni would've been quite happy to stay where they were, close together, but he could see a tiny bit of wariness in her face. Not wanting to push her too far out of her comfort zone, he agreed. As they strolled through the now-closed fish market, she pointed out the carvings on the columns, the churches in the various squares, and buildings with grand facades.

The *osteria* she took him to was small and simply furnished, and the menu was chalked up on the board. Bruschetta for antipasti, risotto for the first course, shrimps with grilled vegetables and polenta for second course, and semifreddo for dessert. There were no choices; clearly the chef was cooking what had been picked up at the market that morning.

It turned out to be the best food he'd ever eaten.

'Told you,' she said. 'The best food is cooked simply and done well.'

'I knew the seafood would be good in Venice,' he said, 'but these shrimps are incredible.' Simply served with olive oil and a squeeze of lemon juice, they were sublime.

'This is Venice at her best,' Serafina said softly, and he had to agree.

The blue hour, the few minutes after the sun had set and when everything was hazy, was one of

Serafina's favourite times. On the way back to the palazzo, Gianni seemed entranced by the changing colour of the water in the canal and the way the light reflected on it. Just as she'd hoped he would be.

'Let's have a glass of wine on the balcony,' she said when they got to the palazzo. 'I know I keep dragging you out there, but the view...' She spread her hands. 'It's my favourite in the whole world.'

'I think even if it was dull and raining, it'd be stunning,' he said. 'Every time I look out, something different catches my eye. A roof or a door or a window or a dome.'

'And it changes with the light,' she said.

'"The reflections from the lights in the buildings look like stars on the water. Heaven on earth",' he quoted when they took their wine outside and settled on the balcony. 'That's what you told me back in Rome.'

'And now you can see it for yourself,' she said.

He inclined his head in acknowledgement. 'At the time, I thought you were being a bit too poetic. But you were right. The lights reflected in the canal really do look like stars.'

It sounded as if he was starting to fall in love with her city.

Tomorrow, she'd show him buildings to take his breath away and make him fall in love even more deeply; but for now she wanted to get to know him better. Find out what made him tick.

Once they were settled on the balcony with a glass of wine, she turned to him. 'Did you always know you were going to be a builder?'

'Like my dad, you mean?' he asked. 'Probably. I used to follow him around all the time. I had a set of wooden building bricks, and he taught me how to make arches and bridges that would bear the weight of my toy cars or my little sister's toy horses. I pestered him to let me help him at work, until finally he gave in and let me help him mix mortar on a Saturday morning. I wasn't even ten when I built my first wall. He taught me to keep my tools clean and always be polite to the client.' He smiled. 'He was right. You catch more flies with honey than you do with vinegar.'

It was obvious that he'd loved his father deeply, the same way that she'd loved hers. Though Serafina hoped that Gianni had been spared her own experience of learning that the father she'd adored was very far from perfect. 'And you joined him in the family business?'

'There wasn't a family business when I was very young,' Gianni said. 'He worked for someone else. But then the construction market went through a bad patch, and he was made redundant. He was out of work for quite a while. He swore he'd never rely on someone else again and he started working for himself. He did little jobs and repairs at first, and then people asked him to build their extensions, and then houses—and then he was employing his own team, tendering for commercial projects.' He looked at her. 'He said you always knew when people had saved up for a job, because they treated you well and appreciated what you did, always made you a drink and let you use their toilets.'

Serafina had a nasty feeling where he was going with this. 'And rich people didn't?'

'If you're doing a job for someone rich, you soon learn to take your own hot drink with you and find out where the nearest public toilet is,' Gianni said dryly.

She flinched inwardly. Was that how her dad had treated anyone who'd done a job for them?

Then again, her family was no longer rich.

And the very first thing she'd done when Gianni had walked through her door was to offer him a hot drink.

Did he know how poor she was? She suspected he'd checked her out on the internet, just as she'd checked him out. Which meant he'd know about Tom. And a journalist somewhere would no doubt have dug up at least some of the dirt on her father.

'For the record,' he said softly, 'not everyone fits their boxes.'

She wasn't even sure what her box was, any more. 'Were you close to your dad?'

'I loved him very much,' he said. 'Though we didn't see things the same way. We didn't agree on the way forward for the business. He liked modern architecture and concrete, especially after building the town hall at Bardicello changed our lives. Though I always hated that building.' His eyes were shadowed when he added, 'And it broke him when it went wrong. It's what caused his heart attack. The one that killed him.'

Just as her own father's bad news had caused his heart attack. She and Gianni weren't so far apart, then. Both had loved their father dearly; both had lost him to a heart attack after bad news. 'I'm so sorry,' she said. 'It's hard when you lose your dad. As if a bit of you has been broken off.'

He nodded. 'And it's the stuff you didn't have time to sort out that hurts the most.'

'All the things you wish you'd said—the things you wish *they'd* said,' she agreed.

His eyes darkened. 'And you have to come to terms with the regrets, the way you feel you disappointed them, because you can't change anything.'

He, too, felt like the child who'd let their parent down? She reached across and squeezed his hand briefly. 'You're the first person I've met who really understands that.'

'Same with you,' he said. 'I mean, my sister gets it, but she didn't clash with our dad the way I did.' He looked at her. 'Though I least I have her. There's just you.'

'Just me,' she said. 'But I'm getting there.' She hoped. 'What actually happened at Bardicello?' she asked. 'I thought concrete was supposed to last for centuries—look at all the undersea ruins divers have found. Or is that why they were ruins?'

'Concrete does last for centuries,' he said. 'And not only in ruins. I assume you know the Pantheon?'

'It's my second favourite building in Rome, after the Colosseum,' she said.

'My dad took me to see it when I was tiny, and he told me it was made of concrete. It's still the world's largest unreinforced concrete dome. And that,' he said, 'is the key word. *Unreinforced.* If the Romans had reinforced their dome with steel, the structure would've collapsed a long time ago.'

'Why is reinforcement a problem?'

'Steel's made from iron, so it rusts. A hundred years ago, everyone thought reinforced concrete was the answer to everything. Steel adds strength, meaning you can have thinner structures which look more attractive, plus they're cheaper and faster to build. Concrete's alkaline, which should inhibit rust, and steel and concrete have similar thermal expansion profiles so there's less chance of cracking.' He paused. 'That's the theory. The buildings were meant to last for a thousand years.'

'And in practice?'

'The steel corrodes. You can't see it deteriorating until it's too late and the concrete's damaged. It's part of the reason I don't use reinforced concrete: the corrosion and the fact that there's a huge carbon footprint.' He grimaced. 'Most of my fights with my dad were over concrete. It kind of got worse after my degree. He thinks—thought—architects were dreamers and pen-pushers.'

'Your degree's in architecture?' she asked.

'No. Building engineering. I knew how things worked; I wanted to know *why*,' he said. 'My dad didn't see the point of studying. He thought I should concentrate on the practical side of building instead of mooning about over the theory.'

It made Serafina realise how lucky she'd been; her family had been happy for her to study whatever she wanted, and had made no protest about her studying for her first degree in Rome rather than in Venice. Gianni had clearly had to fight to get what he wanted.

His next words confirmed it. 'We had endless rows over it, and I was pretty near to walking out of the family firm. In the end, Mamma and

Flora—my sister—made us both see reason. We compromised that I'd do the degree alongside my job.'

He'd admitted earlier that there were clashes between himself and his dad, but this was ridiculous. 'Studying and working full-time in tandem? That's a pretty heavy workload.'

He shrugged. 'It was a compromise that meant we both got our own way. But it also meant I argued with him more. Whenever I tried to persuade him to take the company in a different direction, he said I was becoming a pen-pusher instead of a builder.'

That had clearly hurt; unable to stop herself, she squeezed his hand again. 'It's always good to look at things from another angle.'

'I just wish…'

'He'd understood you more? Confided in you? Let you shoulder some of the burden?' The things she'd wished for from her own father.

'Yeah. It's hard to separate the guilt, the anger and the regrets from the love. And I *miss* him,' he said. 'It's been two years; but, even now, there are things I see or hear that I'd love to share with him, and it hurts like hell that I can't.'

'Me, too,' she said. 'Are you close to your mum and your sister?'

He nodded. 'Flora and I run the company together. She handles finance and the office, and

I handle the construction side. We trust each other's judgement.'

Would she have to convince Flora, too, before Gianni could restore the palazzo? 'Sorry. If I'd realised, I would have invited your sister to visit, too. And your mother. I apologise.' She grimaced. 'I didn't do my research thoroughly enough.'

'You didn't need to invite them. Flora trusts my professional judgment. And finances aren't the only thing to influence whether we take on a project.' He gave her a rueful smile. 'Mamma and Flora have been nagging me for months to take time off. When I told them I was coming to Venice, they were all for it. Apparently I have to take a selfie outside a mask shop, on a gondola, and in a glass-blowing place and send them to them—as proof that I'm not spending all my time measuring things, taking samples and clambering about in attics or squinting at joinery.'

'I'll take the photos for you,' she said with a smile.

'You don't mind me changing your list of things you wanted to show me?'

'They were on it anyway,' she said. 'Though there's a lot more to Venice than masks, gondolas and glass.'

'Noted,' he said. 'But I need to see the touristy bits because I also want to buy a present for my niece.' He smiled. 'Sofia's four.'

'How about a teddy bear with a bridal veil made from Burano lace?' she suggested.

'Possibly yes to a teddy, but maybe not the lace. Our Sofia's not a girly girl,' Gianni said. 'According to Flora, that's her Tio Gi's fault, for teaching her how to make sand wet enough to build with and buying her a toy toolkit for her third birthday instead of a doll's house.' He grinned. 'But if you're going to build a sandcastle, you don't want it to fall down before you've even filled the second bucket of sand. And, the way I see it, if her passion is for building, it's my job as her uncle to support that. Girls can be builders as well as boys.'

Clearly Gianni was very much loved by his family, and Serafina felt a twinge of envy. Her father had loved her, but not enough to trust her with the true state of the family finances; and her mother was so wrapped up in doom and gloom that Serafina trod on eggshells around her most of the time. The only people to nag her about relaxing more was were her aunt Vittoria and her best friend.

'A teddy bear with a gondolier outfit, then,' she said.

'A girl gondolier?'

'*Gondoliera*,' Serafina said. 'Though there are less than a handful of them.'

'Why?' He looked at her. 'You told me you can

drive a boat. Women can drive cars. Why can't a woman be a gondolier? Do you need extra strength to manoeuvre a gondola, or something?'

'I think it's mainly tradition,' Serafina said. 'Fathers tend to hand the business down to their sons. There's a course, and a potential gondolier has to pass exams on local knowledge as well as proving they can manoeuvre a boat. There are less than half a dozen new gondoliers each year.'

'There's still no reason why women can't be gondoliers.'

Serafina liked the way he saw things. If she was honest with herself, she liked *him*. 'I agree. A job appointment should be based on your ability and skills, and nothing else.'

'Absolutely.' He lifted his glass in a silent toast. 'What are the plans for tomorrow?'

'I know you need to do more assessment in the house, but I want to take you to San Marco for breakfast in the oldest coffee house in the world, and then visit the Palazzo Ducale. I think you'll enjoy it.' She'd enjoy it, too.

'I look forward to it,' he said.

She kept the rest of their conversation light until they'd finished the wine.

'I need to catch up on a few emails, if you don't mind.'

'Of course.'

'I'll see you in the morning, then,' he said.

'We'll leave at eight, if that's OK,' she said. 'Feel free to make yourself coffee if you're up earlier.'

'Thank you.' He smiled. 'Goodnight, Serafina. And thank you for a lovely dinner.'

CHAPTER FIVE

GIANNI SLEPT WELL, and was awake ridiculously early. He showered, dressed, and went into the kitchen to make himself a coffee. He thought about making one for Serafina, but he was wary of knocking on her bedroom door. They didn't know each other well enough for him to be comfortable doing that, plus strictly speaking she was a potential client. He'd seen too many examples of people mixing business with pleasure and ending up in a mess.

While he waited for the coffee machine to finish making his coffee, he looked at his surroundings.

This didn't feel like a home.

His mother's kitchen had Sofia's drawings held on to the fridge with magnets, a calendar with reminders and a grocery list. Flora's kitchen was the same. Even his own was decorated with drawings his niece had made for him, with *Ti amo Tio Gi* written across the top in her wobbly handwriting. This kitchen was like that of a show home, with nothing personal on view. No photographs, no postcards, no notes of any description.

No, not a show home, he amended. A museum.

And Contessa Serafina Ardizzone was the last of her line, held here like a pinned butterfly in a frame.

She clearly loved the palazzo, but to him it felt like a mausoleum. All the disapproving portraits, the dust-sheeted furniture, the rooms that had been shut off for decades. The mustiness.

She'd told him that her mother worried. He rather thought that the palazzo would make his own very capable, no-nonsense and bustling mother start to worry, too. The place was oppressive. A burden.

Would it squash Serafina beneath its weight?

He found the tin of sugar and added half a spoonful to his cup, set his mug on the kitchen table, then fetched the file he'd started yesterday and started working through the figures. He was making notes when Serafina walked into the kitchen.

'Good morning,' she said.

She was wearing jeans today, he noticed. Faded ones which hugged her curves, teamed with a strappy top and canvas shoes. She'd taken her hair out of the plait and it fell in waves to her shoulders; shockingly, he found himself wanting to twirl the ends round his fingers.

'Good morning,' he said. 'I did think about making you some coffee when I made mine, but I didn't want to…' He struggled to find the right word. 'Intrude.'

'Coffee is never an intrusion,' she said with a bright smile. 'Did you sleep well?'

'Yes, thanks,' he said, 'though it felt very odd this morning, not hearing any traffic noise.'

'After growing up here, it took me almost a month to get used to the traffic noise when I was a student in Rome—and it was always strange for a few days when I came home,' she said. 'Are you nearly ready for breakfast?'

'Sure.' He closed the file. 'I'll just put this away.'

'I'll grab something to cover my shoulders,' she said.

It was still early enough that not many people were about; Serafina led him through narrow alleyways and across bridges, stopping to point out buildings she thought he'd like along the way.

'We can come back to the shops later,' she said. 'There's a good toy shop nearby.'

'I'm in your hands,' he said.

Then she led him through an archway and stopped talking, letting him drink in his surroundings. He'd seen photographs, but he hadn't been prepared for the sheer grandeur of St Mark's Square in person. There had been little squares on the way here, but he'd got used to narrow passage-ways and canals everywhere, every bit of space used to the full. Even the gardens were vertical, here.

And now suddenly there was space.

A huge rectangular space, with buildings with elegant arcades and columns bounding three sides of it. On the fourth side, he recognised the iconic view of St Mark's Basilica with its onion-shaped domes, the glittering gold mosaics in its arches and the loggia with the four bronze horses. Soaring up into the sky was the slender brick *campanile* with its green triangular roof; and then he could see the Doge's Palace with its graceful arcades, gothic quatrefoils and pink and white walls.

'That's stunning,' he said, enthralled.

She looked pleased. 'Isn't it just? Up close, the carvings on the columns are fabulous. I hoped you'd like this.'

'I do. A lot,' he said. He itched to explore. More than that, he itched to explore—with her right by his side.

She shepherded him towards one of the cafés; tables were set up outside. 'Would you prefer to sit inside or out here?'

'Out here, if you don't mind,' he said. 'That's a view not to be missed.'

The waiter seated them and brought the menu;

they ordered coffee and pastries, then sat back and enjoyed the sunshine, watching the square come to life. The coffee was good, as were the pastries.

'Shall I take a picture for your mother?' she asked.

'To prove to her that I'm idling, not working? Thanks, that'd be kind.' He flicked into his phone's camera app and handed it to her.

'Smile,' she directed, and took a snap before handing the phone back.

He took a snap of the basilica and sent both photos to his mother and his sister, along with a message.

Having breakfast in St Mark's Square. Nice view.

They didn't need to know that the nicer view was Serafina Ardizzone.

Within seconds the replies came back, telling him to relax and have fun. He laughed. 'I'm under strict orders to enjoy myself.' It was hard not to, when the sun was shining and he was having breakfast with someone he was starting to like very much indeed.

'Venetian architecture and Venetian food are excellent. Of course you're going to enjoy yourself,' she said.

He filled in the third excellent Venetian thing for himself: the company of a certain *contessa*.

'Is it a trick of the light, or are two of the columns actually a different colour?' he asked, gesturing to the Doge's Palace.

'Two of them are pink. It's where the Doge stood during official ceremonies, where death sentences were announced and where aristocrats were executed and their bodies displayed as a warning not to plot against the state,' she explained.

'Gory,' he said. 'But, given the gladiators and prisoners in the Colosseum, I can hardly claim the moral high ground.'

'That's my favourite building in Rome,' she said.

'Mine's the Pantheon,' he said. 'Because of the dome.' He smiled. 'I wrote a paper on domes as part of my degree. It was a good excuse to climb inside St Peter's in the Vatican and Brunelleschi's Duomo in Florence.' He looked speculatively at her. 'Can you climb inside any of the domes at St Mark's?'

'Unfortunately not,' she said, 'but the mosaics mean they're pretty spectacular viewing. We could go in for quick look before we go to the Doge's Palace, if you like.'

'That'd be good,' he said. 'Thank you.' He excused himself to go to the bathroom, intending to quietly pay for their breakfast, but discovered that she'd already beaten him to it.

'Thank you for breakfast,' he said when he returned to the square. 'I had planned to treat you.'

She smiled. 'My pleasure. You can buy me lunch. And we're having *tramezzini*.'

'Fine by me,' he said. 'Come and show me your favourite bit of the Basilica.'

'That's the mosaic floor,' she said promptly. 'It's like a sea—not only because of the colour, but because it's actually wavy.'

'Was it designed that way?' he asked, intrigued.

'No. The ground beneath has moved over the centuries. I know it's damage that probably ought to be fixed, but it adds to the atmosphere. Oh, and don't miss the peacock mosaic. That's glorious.'

Once they entered the Basilica, they observed the notices and walked round in silence; it felt more like a sultan's palace than a church, with the glittering gold tesserae covering every surface. Gianni looked up at the ceiling of the domes, the way the tiny windows shed little shafts of light onto the mosaics; they were stunning, but they didn't move him half as much as the woman beside him. In the silence, it felt as if it were just the two of them walking through the church, an oddly intimate feeling among the crowds. When she pointed out the wavy floor and the peacock, he could see the delight in her eyes, and he enjoyed the fact that his personal tour guide was sharing something of herself with him: as well as the fact that she seemed to share his love of architecture.

'Why the peacock in particular?' he asked when they were back in the square.

'I think it's the colours of the feathers,' she said. 'Those gorgeous shades of blue and green, with a hint of gold. Kind of like the different colours in the lagoon at different times of day. Family legend says one of my ancestors used to have a tame peacock and it used to strut around on the ground floor.'

Gianni had never seen a peacock outside a zoo, let alone known anyone who kept a peacock as a pet. It was another reminder that Serafina was from a very different world to his own. And yet, when they'd talked about their fathers, they'd been coming from the same place.

'Depending on what happens with the restoration,' she said, 'I might redecorate some of the bedrooms using those colours.'

'They'd look good in a bathroom, too,' he mused. 'A band of glass mosaic tiles. Especially if you decide to add en-suite bathrooms to the bedrooms you redecorate.'

'I like that idea. Glass, like the tesserae in the Basilica.' She smiled. 'Are you quite sure you're not really an architect at heart?'

'No. I'm a building engineer,' he said. 'I'm the

one who turns the dream into a reality. And not all architects are good when it comes to reality. My dad loved Frank Lloyd Wright's designs, but those cantilevers...' He shook his head. 'For them to work, the builders had to do a bit of finessing.'

'You said you wrote a paper on domes. Have you ever built one?'

'No. Maybe one day,' he said.

'If you could build anything you like,' she asked, 'what would it be?'

Could he tell her? Would she think he was crazy? Or was she open-minded enough to get what had fascinated him, this last year?

'I've been reading interesting things about acoustics,' he said.

'So you'd want to build a concert hall with a dome?' she guessed.

'No. A living space,' he said. 'Because sounds in a building affect the way you feel and the way you react to things. Think of the way an echoing corridor can make you feel uncomfortable, or a bathroom can make your singing sound better.'

'And a dome can do that?'

'Curved ceilings can,' he said. 'Studies show that particular sound frequency affects brain activity. Build your room the right shape, and it can help you concentrate, or calm down.'

'You can actually do that with space?' she asked, looking intrigued. 'When I'm working on

an exhibition, I look at the light in a space and the
way people will move round it, so I can arrange
the art to show it off properly. I never considered
sound. Could the shape of the exhibition space
and the way it reflects sound enhance people's
enjoyment of what they're seeing?'

'That's maybe stretching it a little,' he said, 'but
it's an interesting idea.'

'I'd love to see research on that. Can you give
me any links to papers?' she asked. 'So I can see
where it might fit in with my ground floor?'

She clearly didn't think he was weird or nerdy,
the way Elena had when he'd talked about the
theory of building. Serafina seemed to be as interested by the ideas as he was, and it made him
feel warm inside. Gianni never felt in tune with
someone else like this before; given that they were
from such different backgrounds, she was the last
person he'd expected to understand what made
him tick. 'When we get back to the palazzo,' he
promised. 'I have notes on my laptop. I'll show
you what I've been reading.'

He loved the architecture of the entrance to the
Doge's Palace, and he enjoyed listening to Serafina telling him about the art, including the largest oil painting in the world in the Chamber of
the Great Council.

'Is Tintoretto your favourite artist?' he asked.

'No. That's either Carriera or Titian,' she said.

'I can take you to see my favourite painting in Venice, later in the week. If you want to, that is,' she added swiftly.

'As long as it's not modern art,' he said. 'I'm really not keen on the kind of blobs and squiggles anyone can make if they fling paint at a canvas.'

She laughed. 'As an art historian, I should perhaps stick up for abstract art. The point of it is about how it makes you feel, not how it looks.'

'Maybe I'm uncultured, because it irritates me,' he said. 'But this sort of stuff…' He gestured to the painting. 'There's so much in it. All the little details and meanings. You make it come to life when you tell me the stories behind it. I really like that.'

'It's a delight showing someone who actually gets it,' she said.

Maybe Serafina's ex—despite being an actor—hadn't shared her love of art and hadn't been interested enough to find out what mattered to her, Gianni thought. He was glad she hadn't actually married the man; he hated to think of her moving from a palazzo that threatened to stifle her to a lifestyle that would *definitely* have stifled her.

Gianni Leto was full of surprises, Serafina thought. She'd never considered how the acoustics of buildings could affect people, apart from noise making it hard to concentrate. He'd made her see space in a different way.

And he seemed to understand how she felt about art. Unlike Tom, he wasn't bored by the paintings and only interested in their monetary value. He'd asked questions about little details that Tom would never have noticed; and he'd approached the art in a very different way, asking about the way canvases were constructed and how they were built to fit a particular space. And he listened to her answers instead of glazing over. The intensity of his gaze made her spine tingle with pleasure.

Once they'd finished at the Doge's Palace, she took him shopping.

'Sofia will love this,' he said, picking up a teddy bear dressed as a gondolier in one of the shops. 'And I'd like to get some glass for my mother and my sister.'

'Wait until we go to Murano,' she advised. 'You can see the glass being blown as well.'

'More photo opportunities to prove I'm being idle,' he said with a grin. 'Bring it on.'

She enjoyed showing him her favourite places, including the bookshop where the books were kept in a gondola and bathtubs, meaning they'd float and not be damaged when the high tides flooded the city. And she enjoyed introducing him to *tramezzini*, the overfilled triangular sandwiches that were the city's speciality.

They spent most of the afternoon in a restored palazzo, so Gianni could see how Ca' d'Ardizzone might have looked in the eighteenth century.

'This is the place I was hoping to visit,' he said, looking pleased. 'I know they're lower down here than in your part of the city, but I want to see how they deal with the water, close up.'

He took plenty of photographs on the ground floor, particularly of the water gate; and he spent time talking to the curators, borrowing a tape measure from them. 'You asked me if you could do anything to help,' he reminded her, and waved the tape measure at her.

She'd never visited a museum and taken its measurements before. But she understood why he needed the information; watching him work and seeing the concentration on his face fascinated her.

She knew he was in charge of Leto Construction now, but would he still get a chance to do the hands-on work he clearly loved? The way he'd spoken about working with his dad when he was young: she could imagine him now, working on her house, his hands sure and capable. And from there it was an easy step to imagining his hands touching her, that little pleat of concentration on his brow as he traced the curve of her face with his fingertips, then drew the pad of his thumb across her lower lip...

Oh, for pity's sake. This wasn't about her and Gianni. It was about her palazzo.

But she couldn't push the thought out of her head. She was really aware of him and the way he moved; when his fingers accidentally brushed against hers it felt as if she'd been galvanised.

He'd clearly made a hit with the curators, because when he returned the tape measure they gave him the phone number of the restoration team's office.

'Thank you,' he said. When he and Serafina went up to the next floor, to see the restored rooms, he turned to her. 'Is there a good chocolate shop nearby? Because they've been very helpful and I want to show my appreciation.'

She liked the fact that he wasn't the kind of man who took someone for granted. He was sure of himself without being arrogant, and he listened as much as he talked. If her situation was different, she'd be tempted to start dating him.

But right now her life was a mess, and she couldn't let herself be distracted from her goal. She needed to save the palazzo and save the museum.

'Yes. There's one round the corner,' she said.

'Good.' He studied each room in the restored rooms, taking detailed notes and photographs as they went round. 'I'm going to compare this to your palazzo, later,' he said. 'This has given me an excellent idea of how it would've looked. Though obviously there are differences: you have no frescoes or decorative plasterwork on the walls or ceilings. And the wallpaper here doesn't have damp stains or peel away.'

He certainly wasn't pulling his punches, she thought. She appreciated his honesty; but it didn't sound as if he was anywhere near falling in love with the house, the way she'd hoped he would. She obviously needed to work harder.

'Do you think the staining on the wallpaper is from rising damp, or from something else?' she asked.

'I need to look at the outside of the palazzo to check a few things,' he said, 'but at the moment I think on the ground floor the damp patches might be from a structural problem, and on the *piano nobile* it's a combination of water coming in through rotten parts in the windows and condensation caused by poor ventilation. I looked where the wall-coverings had come away and some of the plaster's crumbling, too. But it's all fixable.'

In one way, that was reassuring; in another, it wasn't, because he hadn't mentioned how much fixing the problems would cost in terms of time and money.

He glanced at his watch. 'We probably should

get back. I'd like to finish assessing the second floor today.'

That was the whole reason why he was here; but Serafina had been enjoying showing him her city, and she felt oddly flat at the idea of stopping. And she was cross with herself when she realised that it wasn't so much showing off her beloved Venice that she'd enjoyed; it had been spending time with Gianni that had made her feel so bright. 'Of course,' she said politely.

He bought chocolates to thank the curators; they went all fluttery over him, and Serafina didn't want to examine quite why that irritated her. But she was definitely feeling a bit out of sorts by the time they got back to her palazzo.

'I want to look at the outside,' he said when she unlocked the back door. 'Can I get access to the outside of the building through the second water gate?'

'I'll need to find the key,' she said.

'I'll continue working on the second floor,' he said. 'Come and get me when you've found the key.'

Serafina found five possible keys, but none of them would turn in the lock. 'I can't even remember the last time we used that door. It's probably seized up. Should I get some oil for the lock?' she asked Gianni.

'No. That's a myth, because what happens is

that dust sticks to the oil and makes it worse. You need a dry lubricant,' he said. It was obvious that she didn't have a clue what he meant, because he smiled and said, 'We'll improvise.' He took a multi-tool from his pocket and whittled a pencil, leaving a long length of lead, and shoved it into the lock.

'Isn't that going to make it worse?' she asked, when the lead broke.

'Not once I've jiggled the key enough to grind it up. Dry lubricant is powdered graphite, and that's what we'll end up with,' he said.

It took a few goes, but eventually he was able to open the lock and inspect the wall outside.

'And this is what I thought I'd find,' he said, showing her the crumbling brickwork; there were cracks in the mortar. 'When the levels rise in the canal, the water comes through here. Bricks are porous. Rainwater's fine, but salt water tends to cause damage, particularly when the water goes upwards. You might need to replace some of the bricks as well as the mortar. And you need lime mortar, because it's porous.'

'But you just said being porous is the problem.'

'Not for mortar, because it means the water evaporates easily. Modern cement mortar traps moisture; the water can't escape through the mortar, so it moves to the surface of the bricks. As soon as there's frost, the water freezes, and the brick starts crumbling. That's what you can see here.'

'I think I'm beginning to see why my ancestors ignored the problems,' she said with a sigh. 'It's a lot easier than worrying about whether you can fix them.'

'It's all fixable,' he said.

'But you're going to give me a huge list of things that need doing, aren't you?'

'That,' he said, 'was the whole point of my visit, was it not? You needed an honest list of what the problems are—and that includes the things you'll need a specialist to look at.'

'Specialist?' She felt her eyes widen.

'For the electrics and the plumbing, which I'm not qualified to assess,' he said. 'But, once you have your list, you can put the tasks in priority order and work through them.'

'Which I guess is a bit like setting up an exhibition,' she said.

'It's the same with any project. Rome wasn't built in a day, and neither was Venice. Or even this house. You have to break it down and do some critical path analysis,' he said. 'List what needs to be done, how long it takes, and what tasks impact on others. Nothing's impossible. You need to find the right way to approach it, and break it down into smaller steps where you can.'

He made it sound really easy. And she'd coordinated plenty of projects over the years. She knew she was good at organising.

So why did this suddenly feel horribly daunting?

Probably because it didn't only affect her, any more. It affected the future of the museum, too.

'I need coffee,' she muttered. And preferably her bodyweight in *bussolai*.

He rested his hand briefly on her shoulder. 'Breathe,' he said softly. 'You're perfectly capable of sorting this out.'

She wasn't sure what warmed her most: his faith in her, or the touch of his hand through the cotton shirt she'd used as a jacket. Not many people in her life had really believed in her: her best friend, her aunt, her boss, and sometimes her dad. Support from such an unexpected source made her heart skip a beat. Gianni seemed to see who she was, beneath the title and the glitz: the person who did actually *do* the hard work, even when it was a struggle. And that bolstering really helped with the ridiculous wobble in her confidence.

'If I can be cheeky,' he added, 'I'd love a coffee, please. I need to do some measuring and take some photographs out here. I'll lock up when I'm done.'

In other words, he didn't want her under his feet, getting in the way and distracting him with a gazillion questions. And hadn't she promised not to micromanage? 'I'll sort the coffee,' she said.

Once she'd delivered a mug of coffee to him, she took the photograph albums and a pad of sticky notes out to the balcony, and went through them, marking the useful pages.

Eventually he came out to join her. 'OK. That's three floors and the outside done. Just the top floor and any attic space to go. I'm assuming you do have a ladder to get up to the attic space so I can check the inside of the roof?'

'Somewhere,' she said. She hadn't been up there for years. 'It's most probably in the room with the trap door. I'll check before we go out tonight. If I can't find it, I'll borrow one.' She bit her lip. 'How bad is it?'

'Apart from the things I've already told you about, you have a bit of a condensation problem. I'd recommend having an extractor fan fitted in the kitchen and bathrooms. In the meantime, keep the door closed and the window open to stop the condensation spreading to the rest of the palazzo, especially when you dry clothes,' he said. 'You've done the right thing, keeping the doors closed for the rooms you've shut off; but you also need to ventilate them properly. And you'll need to make a decision about the wall-covering: whether you conserve some of it on a feature wall, repair the damaged bits, or take it all down. Obviously that depends,' he said, 'on what you intend to do with the rooms.'

'Shabby chic isn't going to cut it,' she said with a sigh.

'You might be able to get away with the furniture,' he said. 'But definitely not the plumbing, the electrics or the bits that need repair. That wall-covering's going to have to come off anyway, so the electrics can be replaced—though that's also good for you, because you can make sure you have enough sockets.' He glanced at the albums on the table next to her. 'From those sticky notes, do I take it you found something?'

'I did.' She opened the first page. 'You wanted early photographs. These are my great-great-great-grandparents in the ballroom at the end of the eighteen-hundreds. My great-great-great-grandfather's here in the library, and here in the family gondola. And these are my great-great-great-grandparents in the drawing room giving dinner parties.' She gave him a wry smile. 'That might have been the real Canaletto, back then.' But had the partying been a way of dealing with all the tensions in her great-great-great-grandparents' marriage, just as her mother's doom-and-gloom and her father's gambling had been their way of dealing with it?

'This is fascinating,' he said sitting next to her and looking at the albums with her. 'This would be before electricity was installed—and definitely before your heating was put in.'

'I'm guessing the radiators need updating. I have to bleed them a lot,' she said.

'I'm not surprised. Your plumbing needs work, too.'

'Is *anything* about the house OK?' she asked, wincing inwardly as she heard the plaintiveness in her tone.

She sounded so forlorn. Gianni wanted to wrap his arms round her and tell her everything was going to be all right—that he'd make it all right—but how could he? It wasn't his place to hold her. But he could at least reassure her from a professional point of view. 'The structure of the palazzo is reasonable, given its age,' he said. 'Yes, there are problems, but they can be fixed. Though now is your chance to be radical. to make it the home you want it to be.'

'What would you do with it, if it was yours?' she asked.

'To make it pay for itself and be used? I'd turn the top two floors into apartments,' he said, 'and rent them out; then it would be full of people instead of silence. I'd remodel this floor for personal use, with good en-suite bathrooms and decent heating, add extra plug sockets during the rewiring so you have enough to suit a modern lifestyle, and partition some of the rooms to maximise their use. I'd definitely get rid of the wall-covering.' He saw her flinch, and said gently, 'Donate it to a museum, because it's not doing you any favours here. It's damaged, and reproducing what you have here is going to be costly and take a lot of time. If it was mine, I'd replaster the walls and add a bit of plaster detail—doing it the same way they would've done at the time the palazzo was built—and then paint it.'

She looked aghast. 'That means you'd lose the history.'

'A compromise. I'd bring it back to life. Make it a proper home.' And he could see it: a comfortable, bright space. Though he wasn't entirely sure whether the brightness was because of the palazzo itself or because of the woman who stood before him. He spread his hands. 'You did ask. If you want to live in a museum on all four floors, sticking with the choices of the people who came before you, that's your call. But for me a home reflects the people who live in it. It's where they can be themselves.'

She didn't look convinced.

Well, he'd started now. He might as well push it a bit more. 'Your library. Your office. Do you ever sit in those big leather chairs and read or listen to music?'

'No,' she admitted.

'Then maybe,' he said, 'you need to go through the furniture. Sell the stuff you don't use or don't love, or donate it to a museum, and bring in stuff that works for you. Being the custodian of a place doesn't mean you can't ever change things. It means you can add your own layer to the history.'

She looked thoughtful. 'I'd never considered that.'

'It's something to add in to your renovation plans,' he said. 'Spend a while thinking about what *you* want.'

'Maybe.' She glanced at her watch. 'It's too late to climb the stairs today, but I'd like to show you a tower on the way to dinner.'

'Dinner which I'm paying for,' he said swiftly, 'given that you bought me dinner last night.'

'You're my guest. We'll argue later,' she said.

They wouldn't argue, because Gianni knew a quick way to circumvent any disputes. Though he appreciated the fact that, unlike his ex, Serafina didn't expect him to pick up all the bills simply because he was rich. 'I need to dust off and change,' he said. 'I'll be quick.'

'Me, too,' she said.

When he emerged from his room, she was wearing another of those pretty, floaty summer dresses. He wondered if she had any idea how stunning she was. Though it wasn't only her looks that attracted him. It was Serafina herself: her energy, her brightness.

She took him through a maze of alleyways. 'This is Scala Contarini del Bovolo. It's at its best in the evening light.'

'I can see why they called it a snail shell, having the spiral visible on the outside as well as the inside,' he said. 'I like it very much.'

'Maybe we can climb it later in the week,' she said. 'It's unusual in being one of the high places in Venice where you can't actually see any water from the top.'

'Though the tower isn't quite as tall as it looks,' he said.

She looked surprised. 'How do you mean?'

'They're using an architectural trick,' he said. 'Every layer you go up, the loggias decrease in size.'

'I've lived in Venice all my life—apart from my three years in Rome—and I never realised that,' she said.

'Just as I'm sure you could show me things in Rome I didn't know about,' he said with a smile.

When she took him to another *osteria,* not far from St Mark's Square, Gianni took the precaution of handing his credit card over at the beginning of the evening, to make quite sure he picked up the bill without having to argue with her.

They ate scallops first, served with good bread

to mop up the garlicky juices, and a bone-dry white wine. He enjoyed the meal, but even more he enjoyed Serafina's company. For someone who'd lived a public life, as the former girlfriend of a movie star, he thought she was a very private person, giving little away about herself. The nearest she'd come to opening up was where art or her house were concerned.

She was talking about her balcony when she said, 'It's a good place to paint.' And then she looked shocked, as if she hadn't meant to let that slip out.

'You're an artist as well as an art historian?' he asked, intrigued.

'Not really. I paint just for me. For fun.'

'What sort of thing do you paint? People, animals, landscapes?' Then he remembered her comments about modern art. 'Or is it the sort of abstract stuff I insulted?'

She smiled, then. 'No, it's realist rather than abstract—and I paint Venice. The canal. Water and sky and light.' She wrinkled her nose. 'And my house. Little details. I did a pen and ink sketch that Alessia thinks would make a perfect label.'

'Label?'

'She has this mad idea that I should turn the house into a gin palazzo and use the downstairs as a warehouse and distillery.'

'A gin palazzo.' He grinned. 'Oh, I love that. It's inspired.'

'It's not practical. You can't just buy a still and make some gin. You have to work out your recipe and test the botanicals, trial and error, until you get the right blend. Plus commercial production means expensive equipment and employing a good distiller.'

'It sounds as if you've looked into it.'

'Not quite. Alessia wrote a feature on gin, and she made me go with her to help her taste-test stuff,' she explained.

He smiled. 'Tough job, but someone had to do it?'

She smiled back. 'Exactly. When I was saying that I need the house to pay its way, she came up with the idea of making craft gin.'

'It might be worth costing it out properly,' he said. 'On the upside, you wouldn't have to worry about guests being upset by the mess and noise of the restoration of the other floors. And it might make you more money than the museum can pay you.'

'I thought about it,' she said. 'But the ground floor is definitely going to be an exhibition space.'

'Why?'

She shook her head. 'I can't discuss that.'

'Can't or won't?'

'Can't.' She raked her hand through her hair. 'Right now, all I can tell you is that I have a suitable space and I know an organisation that could use it.'

He appreciated the fact that she wouldn't break a confidence. And he wasn't going to push her on it. Instead, he took the conversation back to something light, talking about movies and Rome, things they had in common. She persuaded him to try the tiramisu, which she said was the best in the city. And they lingered over coffee, just talking.

It wasn't a proper date, but in a weird way it felt like one. Serafina was the first woman since Elena had dumped him to make him actually want a relationship. He knew he'd used work as an excuse, claiming he was too busy to date. It was true; but he also hadn't wanted to risk dating someone, only to find that again he'd picked someone who valued him for his bank balance and didn't see him for who he really was.

He was beginning to think that maybe Serafina was different. Like him, she was shouldering responsibilities; like him, she was struggling to cope with the loss of a parent. And, like him, she kept herself at a slight distance from other people, not quite trusting relationships.

Maybe they could help each other move past the things that held them back.

If he was prepared to take the risk, would she? Or was he deluding himself?

On the way back to palazzo, they walked through St Mark's Square again. It was very different at night, and brighter than he'd expected. Moonlight spilled over the stone paving; there was a lantern in every archway on every floor of the elegant buildings, making it seem magical. The front of the Basilica, too, was lit up, and the golden mosaics sparkled.

There were musicians playing outside one of the cafés—not the endless Vivaldi that Gianni had been expecting, but a show tune he recognised. 'Somewhere' from *West Side Story*: a film he knew well, because it was one of his mother's favourites.

Although there weren't that many people around, a few couples were dancing in the square.

On impulse, he held out his hand to her. 'Dance with me?'

She stared at him as if he'd grown two heads. 'Dance?'

'Sorry. Stupid tourist idea,' he muttered.

'It's not a stupid idea at all. It's been a while since I've danced,' she said.

And the last time she'd danced, he thought, had been with a movie star. How could a mere builder begin to compare—even if he did happen to be the head of a large firm? Plus he couldn't even remember the last time he'd danced.

'Thank you for asking. Yes, I'll dance with you,' she said, and took a step towards him.

Gianni was glad he'd asked her, but regretted it at the same time: because being this close to her really made him aware of her. The way she felt in his arms, the sweet floral scent she wore, the warmth and softness of her skin.

Dancing together for the first time should've been slightly awkward; weirdly, it felt as if they'd done this before. He drew her closer and she rested her cheek against his shoulder When he closed his eyes, he felt as if it could have been only the two of them in the whole wide world. Nothing but them and the music and the moonlight.

Her arms tightened round him.

Somehow they both moved, and they were cheek to cheek.

Another tiny shift, and the corners of their mouths were touching.

He couldn't resist brushing his mouth against hers: a light, sweet touch, exploring rather than demanding. When she kissed him back, tentative and shy, it felt as if fireworks were going off in his head: starbursts of gold and silver.

The next thing he knew, they were kissing properly.

In public.

In the middle of an enormous square with complete strangers around them.

This was something he would normally never do; but something about her made him want this. And more. He wanted to carry her back to her palazzo, carry her up the stairs to his bed, make that mausoleum echo with laughter and joy.

He broke the kiss and stared at her.

Her eyes were huge, mingled desire and joy and worry skittering over her expression. And he could guess why. He'd kissed her. OK, she'd kissed him back, but he'd been the one to cross the line—and he shouldn't have pushed her.

'I'm sorry,' he said, taking a step back. 'I shouldn't...' He shook his head. 'It's no excuse, but this...' He gestured to the square. And the little orchestra seemed to be reading his mind, because now they were playing a jazz tune his grandmother loved: 'You and the Night and the Music'.

He'd never understood that before.

He did now.

'You and the night and the music,' he said helplessly.

'It...we both made a mistake,' she said.

And there were shadows in his eyes that broke his heart. Shadows he rather thought her ex might have put there, because although he hadn't known her for long he was pretty sure she wasn't the sort to cause the problems in a relationship.

'We'll…' She swallowed hard. 'We'll pretend it didn't happen.'

Pretend he hadn't seen fireworks in his head when she'd kissed him back?

Then again, maybe she was right to call a halt. He hadn't been good enough for Elena's family, so how could he possibly be good enough for a *contessa* whose family stretched back centuries and who had the gilt-framed portraits marching up her staircase to prove it? He'd be setting himself up for a fall—again—if he kept up this stupid idea about dating Serafina. Hadn't he learned his lesson that posh women were trouble?

'Of course,' he said.

They walked back to the palazzo in silence. He didn't have a clue what to say; in the end he said nothing, afraid of making the tension between them worse.

The city was quiet apart from the swish of the waves and the gondolas bobbing at their stands. For a moment, Gianni longed for Rome—noisy, uncomplicated Rome with all the cars rushing round. But if he wasn't here, he wouldn't be with Serafina. And it unsettled him that he wanted to be with her more than he wanted to be at home. How had that happened?

'I need to check my emails and sort out some

things for work,' he said as she unlocked the back door. It wasn't strictly true, but it was easier to give a polite fib.

'Sure. See you tomorrow,' she said. 'I hope you don't mind leaving the house at seven? I've planned to take you to the Rialto, and we can have breakfast out.'

'See you tomorrow,' he said. 'Is it OK if I grab a glass of water?'

'Please, treat the house as your home,' she said. 'If you want a drink or a snack, raid the fridge or the larder.'

The stilted conversation felt all wrong, after the way she'd felt in his arms, but he couldn't for the life of him think how to fix this, how to tell her about the weird thoughts spinning through his head. Instead, he took refuge in small talk. 'Thank you. Can I get you anything?'

'No, I'm fine, thanks,' she said, and gave him a super-bright smile.

Cursing himself for being an idiot, Gianni sorted out a glass of water, then went to his room and checked his emails. His team had kept him briefed on what was going on. Some of the project managers had taken decisions without checking with him first, and were clearly enjoying their chance to shine. Good. That was the direction he'd wanted to take the firm in. He wrote supportive replies, then tried to concentrate on working on the report for the palazzo; but he couldn't get

Serafina out of his head. Serafina and the shadows in her eyes. Serafina, who'd made the world vanish with a kiss.

He needed to work out what the barriers were between them—and how he could overcome them.

Serafina went to the library, cross with herself. She should at the very least have offered Gianni somewhere to work. There was a dressing table in his room with a stool, but that wasn't good enough for working. Though she could hardly go and knock on his door right now, could she?

The door to his bedroom.

Her mouth tingled.

No.

Focus, she told herself fiercely. Tomorrow morning, she'd offer him the sitting room or the kitchen table or her library, whichever he'd like most.

She checked her emails. One from Alessia in Florence, where she was interviewing a subject and taking a couple of days out, asking her how things were. One from her aunt, attaching a rare photograph of her mother actually smiling—and how much that lightened Serafina's heart. One from Maddalena, asking how it was going with her assessor and with the new exhibition catalogue, and if there was anything she could do.

She started to reply, but all the words felt jumbled in her head. That kiss had thrown her. It was the first time anyone had kissed her like that in the last year.

And the way Gianni made her feel was like nothing she'd ever experienced before. Dancing with him, she'd felt as if she was floating in the square, and the kiss had increased the floatiness. It had been as if they were dancing under a sky of shooting stars.

When he'd stopped kissing her, she'd realised she was risking making a fool of herself.

She couldn't afford to let anything get in the way of fixing the palazzo and saving the museum. She needed to get things back on an even keel between herself and Gianni, which meant that the attraction she felt towards him would definitely have to be squashed.

Then she looked down at the lined pad next to her laptop and discovered she'd sketched him, without even realising that she'd taken the lid off the gel pen.

Oh, for pity's sake.

This had to stop.

She couldn't afford to take a risk. Relationships didn't work out, in her family. She'd thought she was the one who'd break the cycle, but she'd fallen for a cheat and a liar. Gianni had integrity; but there was simply too much at stake. If she started seeing him and it went wrong, it would mean he wouldn't help her with the palazzo. And that would be disastrous for the museum as well as for the palazzo.

So she'd just have to keep her feelings under control and treat this whole thing as business.

CHAPTER SIX

GIANNI WOKE TO a silent house, turned over in the unfamiliar bed and thought of Serafina.

How was he going to face her this morning?

He knew he shouldn't have kissed her.

Though she *had* kissed him back.

She'd said it was a mistake and they'd agreed it shouldn't have happened; but that had been last night. Today, he still felt out of sorts and fidgety. How would she be with him today? Bright and breezy? Or shy and awkward?

He could ask the same question of himself. How, just how, was he going to face her?

Given how badly things had ended with Elena, he knew this could end up in a huge mess, too. Maybe he should simply tell her he was sorry but he couldn't help her.

Then again, he'd started to fall in love with the palazzo. The idea of turning it from this dust-sheeted, damp and silent place into one that was full of life and people was all too tempting.

And it meant he'd be spending more time with

Serafina. Getting to know her. Letting her get to know him. And maybe, just maybe, that mistake they'd made tonight would change into something else. Something they both wanted.

He couldn't hear any sounds of her moving about, so he judged it would be safe to make himself a coffee. Caffeinated-up, he might have a better idea of how to approach her this morning. After he'd showered, he made himself a mug of instant coffee and went to sit on the balcony: but when he opened the doors he discovered that she was already there, with an empty coffee mug and a sketch pad in front of her. Meaning that she must have been up much earlier than he had.

She looked at him, her dark eyes huge.

This was awkwardness piling upon awkwardness.

'Good morning. About last n—' he began.

At exactly the same time she said, 'Good morning. About last night.'

He stopped. 'Um—you first?'

'I was going to say the same thing,' she said, colour slashing across her cheekbones.

OK. He'd be brave. 'I'm sorry. I crossed a line. I don't want things to be awkward.'

'Me, too,' she said. 'To all of it.'

'Let's put it down to…'

'Propinquity?' she suggested.

'I was going to say the atmosphere.'

'That, too. The music. And Venice at night is…' She spread her hands.

Enchanted. Romantic. A place that could make him forget who he was. 'Yeah.'

'Is that coffee cold enough to chug down?' she asked.

'It will be if I add some cold water. Why?'

'As you're up, we might as well hit the Rialto,' she said. 'I'll buy the makings of dinner at the market. We can grab breakfast at a *pasticceria*. And I think the market right now would be a good photo for your mum.'

'I'll go fix my coffee,' he said.

He added enough cold water to be able to drink it straight down, then let her lead the way to the Rialto.

The market was nothing like the quiet courtyards they'd walked through on Monday. In the early morning, it was full of people. Stallholders in the fish market were using watering cans to water their wares, keeping the fish cool and making them glisten invitingly in the light: everything from soft-shelled crabs to slices of fresh tuna, lobsters to sole. Fishermen were bringing their catch straight from their boats to the tables, to be prepared for customers. Fruit and vegetables were piled high on the stalls in the other part of the market, everything from radicchio to artichokes to tiny wild strawberries, velvet-skinned peaches and fresh herbs. People were talking, bargaining, laughing; old ladies with their shopping trolleys and old men were catching up with their friends, all mingled together with young parents with babies in slings, students, and clearly local people picking up the makings of dinner before going to work.

It was noisy and chaotic, and Gianni loved it. 'It reminds me of the Campo de' Fiori.'

'Venice is *way* better than Rome,' she retorted.

'In your dreams,' he scoffed. 'It was the Roman Empire that ruled the world, not the Venetian one.'

And, just like that, the awkwardness between them had gone, replaced by the camaraderie they'd built before that kiss. He enjoyed watching her haggle for fish, picking out choice pieces. 'I'm cooking fish stew for dinner tonight,' she told him. 'Oh, wait—here's a good spot for a photo for your mum.'

He handed his phone to her, and she took a photograph of him with one of the fish stalls in the background.

'Thanks,' he said.

'Right. I need fennel and thyme,' she said.

Once they'd bought everything on her list—a list, he noticed, that was entirely in her head—they headed over to one of the small bars surrounding the market, ordering coffee and pastries which they ate standing at the bar.

'We'll drop this lot off before we go exploring,' she said.

She showed him a couple of statues on the way; and then, to his surprise, instead of going via the bridge, she took him to the edge of the canal to join a queue.

'We'll cross by *traghetto*,' she said. 'It's a bit like a large gondola, except you stand up for the crossing.'

He eyed the water. 'Stand up?' Was that even safe? Weren't you supposed to sit down on a boat?

And then he could see for himself: a boat was coming towards the quay, with a man standing at each end with large paddles to row the craft across the canal, and the dozen or so people in the centre were all standing up.

Once the passengers had disembarked, the people in their queue began to board.

'Is this what it's like, being in a gondola?' he asked quietly.

'Sort of. Actually, even though this is a touristy thing, I don't think I'm going to take a photo of this for your mum, because you look a bit worried,' she said.

'I'm not used to travelling on the water,' he said. 'Standing up feels…' He wrinkled his nose. 'I guess the first time you went on the Metro in Rome it must've felt as weird for you as this does for me.'

She laughed. 'Just a bit. I'm not used to the underground. We don't have catacombs in Venice, and there aren't even many crypts.'

'Because they flood?' he guessed.

'Exactly.'

Gianni was glad that she chatted to him all the way across the river, and even more glad when they were able to disembark. He hadn't enjoyed the way the gondola had felt as if it were bouncing on the surface of the canal whenever a larger craft went past.

'I had planned a proper gondola trip this evening,' she said. 'Will you be OK, or would you rather skip it?'

'If we're sitting down, I'll be fine,' he said. 'It was only when other boats passed us and made the *traghetto* bob up and down. I could imagine losing my balance, knocking into the other passengers like a domino and making them fall overboard.'

She laughed. 'You were perfectly safe. You're more likely to fall when you're climbing up inside a dome or on a roof somewhere.'

He wasn't convinced but said politely, 'I guess.'

Once Serafina had bought bread from the little bakery round the corner from the palazzo and put the fish in the fridge, she took Gianni out to explore Dorsoduro.

'It's the highest part of the city,' she told him. 'It's very pretty. And there's a shop I think you'll like—at least, your mum will,' she added with a smile.

'No lecture about Venice being more than just masks?' he teased.

'Because then you'll start telling me there's more to Rome than the Colosseum,' she teased back.

When they rounded a corner, a figure wearing a plague doctor mask loomed by the shop doorway.

'Masks. Another to tick off my list,' he said. He duly posed next to the figure so she could take a snap for his mother.

Then she made the mistake of catching his gaze.

She could imagine being at a masked ball with him. Dancing, the way they'd danced in the square last night. And kissing…

Oh, help.

Now her brain was scrambled.

What had she been talking about?

Masks. They were at a mask shop. Of course she was talking about masks. 'I think your mother's going to protest if you send her a snap of you posing outside a shop, but not one of you wearing a mask.'

'Let's go and try one on,' he said.

He put on a Harlequin mask with its distinctive

diamond pattern in red and black and gold; and he looked breathtakingly handsome. At a ball, he'd definitely sweep her off her feet. They'd agreed to pretend last night never happened, but she couldn't put it out of her head.

The way she'd felt when he'd kissed her.

That feeling of floating on air, dissolving into a spiral of desire.

'Now you,' he said.

'Um…'

'Can I pick for you?' he asked.

She nodded and he chose a Columbina mask in deep blue, adorned with a peacock feather.

'It suits you,' he said, and traced her jawline with the tip of his finger. She felt her lips part, inviting him closer.

This was crazy.

It could never work between them. They lived miles apart, they came from different worlds, and they wanted different things. Plus she was an Ardizzone, doomed by an ancient curse that had never let any of her family have a happy relationship.

'Let me take a photo for your mother,' she said, hoping that he wouldn't hear the crack in her voice.

When she'd taken the snap, he said, 'And now one for yours. Smile.'

She let him take the photograph, because it was

easier than explaining why she could never send a picture like that to her mother. Though maybe her aunt or Alessia might like it.

'Are all the masks tied by ribbons?' he asked.

'It's more practical,' she said. 'You can buy ones with a baton so you can hold the mask up to your face—or there's the Moretta mask, traditionally worn by women.' She gestured to the plain black oval face masks. 'They don't quite hide your face; but you hold them in place by biting a button, meaning your voice can't give away your identity.'

'That,' he said, 'sounds utterly ridiculous. You couldn't eat, you couldn't drink, and what if you had a sneezing fit?'

'Agreed. They weren't practical.'

Unlike a certain building engineer.

He bought a Columbina mask with bright red feathers for his niece, and she continued showing him round Dorsoduro.

'I read this was the academic area of Venice,' he said. 'Your museum's near here, isn't it?'

'Yes, but it's not open right now,' she said swiftly. Although part of her wanted to take him to see it, part of her was antsy. There was a fair bit of the kind of modern art she knew he didn't like at the museum; she wanted him only to see things about Venice he'd definitely love rather than something that might make him feel lukewarm about the palazzo restoration. She distracted him from asking her when it would be open by taking him to see a workshop where they repaired gondolas. Thankfully he was interested enough in the construction to drop the subject.

Why was Serafina so keen to keep him away from the museum where she worked? Gianni wondered. Unless *that* was the museum that needed the space at her palazzo. But he had a feeling that, if he asked, she'd stonewall him.

Later that afternoon, back at the palazzo, he assessed the rest of the top floor and wrote up his notes while she made a fish stew.

'How was it?' she asked when he came back into the kitchen.

Her eyes were full of hope. He hated to wreck that; yet, at the same time, he couldn't lie. 'We've got the same window problem, with damp in the plaster where the woodwork has rotted and let water in. And two of the rooms have water damage to the ceiling; either the guttering's failed or there's a problem with your roof.'

He could see her shoulders hunching, absorbing yet another blow, and it made him feel horrible. 'I need to check the attic.'

She nodded. 'I'm calling in a favour from a friend. We can pick up the ladder tomorrow.'

'OK,' he said. And then, because he wanted to

stop her worrying about what he might find, he said, 'Something smells amazing.'

'Thank you. I'm going to start the polenta now. Half an hour until dinner OK with you?'

'Fine,' he said. 'I'm a bit…um…dusty. Do you need a hand with anything, or do you mind if I take a shower?'

'It's fine,' she said. 'I'll see you for dinner.'

The stew and polenta tasted as good as they smelled. But he couldn't take his eyes off her.

When they'd danced together, she'd kissed him back. They were both single. They were from different worlds, yes, but he didn't think she'd be bothered about his poor background; there was none of the snobbery that he'd encountered from Elena's family. He couldn't think of one good reason why they couldn't see where this took them.

But he knew she'd been hurt. Of course she'd be wary. How was he going to persuade her to take a chance on him? Then again, part of him was scared to take a chance on her. He didn't have a clue how to pick his way through the minefield.

She kept the conversation light and sparkly, telling him snippets of the history of Venice and gondolas: all stuff he found interesting. But he was aware that she was wearing a mask: that she was acting the role of hostess.

No, that wasn't fair. She was a good hostess. She was genuinely making him welcome in her home. But she was definitely hiding herself. He couldn't help wondering why—and wondering exactly what she was hiding.

'And now you'll get to see the Grand Canal properly,' she said. 'By gondola.'

'We'll have the guy in a straw boater and stripy jumper singing "O Sole Mio"?' he asked.

'Apart from the fact that's a Neapolitan song, not a Venetian one, the gondoliers concentrate on rowing,' she said. 'Besides, you said you weren't keen on classical music, and the *bacarolles* sung on a gondola are mostly inspired by opera.'

That was true: but part of him felt disappointed. A gondola ride at sunset without someone singing? It didn't feel right.

As if his disappointment showed on his face, she said, 'Actually, I did hire someone to serenade us because I wanted you to have the—well, "Venetian" experience.' She added quote marks with her fingers.

'Even if it means songs from Naples?' he teased.

'Even if.'

She took him down to a gondola stand and introduced him to Franco, their gondolier, and Roberto, who was already seated in the gondola and holding a guitar.

He settled back against the surprisingly comfortable seat next to Serafina, and Franco rowed them along the canal.

'Shall I get *that* one over with, first?' Roberto asked with a grin, and proceeded to sing 'O Sole Mio'; tourists stood watching them on the banks, applauding as they went past.

Serafina took a few seconds of video footage on her phone, of both Roberto and Gianni. 'So your mum knows you did this the traditional way,' she said. 'I'll send it to you later.'

Gianni smiled in acknowledgement. 'Thanks.'

Franco rowed them under the Bridge of Sighs, then took them through a narrow maze of canals. As the light began to fade, Roberto switched to playing a mixture of ballads and short classical pieces Gianni didn't recognise but discovered he actually liked. He found himself relaxing, enjoying the views and the music and the changing colours in the sky.

When they went round a narrow corner, there was a slight jolt and somehow Gianni ended up with his arm round Serafina, steadying her on the seat.

Their eyes met, and colour stole into her face. He could feel his own cheeks heating, too.

He wanted her. Really, really wanted her. Part of him remembered how it had felt to dance with her in St Mark's Square and wanted to draw her closer; but part of him panicked, remembering how much he'd hurt after Elena had dumped him.

Panic won, and he withdrew his arm. 'Safer than being on a roof, right?' he said dryly.

But this wasn't a physical danger, one he knew how to minimise. It was an emotional danger, and he didn't know where to start guarding himself against that. Particularly when Franco steered them back onto the Grand Canal and they had a wonderful view of the sun setting as they sailed under the Rialto, the colours in the sky turning the turquoise waters pink, too.

How easy it would be to kiss her again.

To fall in love with her.

And then would he get his heart broken all over again?

Back at the gondola stand, they said goodbye to Franco and Roberto.

'Thank you,' he said politely to Serafina. 'That was a real treat.'

'You're very welcome. I'm glad you enjoyed it,' she said.

He was tempted to ask her to have a drink with him. To walk hand in hand with him under the darkening skies, watching the lights turn to stars in the canal. To kiss him in the moonlight.

But then things would start to get complicated.

'I'm sorry to be rude,' he said, 'but I need to deal with a couple of things for work.' It wasn't strictly true—they were things that could wait until he was back in Rome next week—and he berated himself for being cowardly enough to use work as an excuse. But with work he knew where he was; with Serafina, his head was all over the place.

'Of course. And I have an exhibition catalogue to finish writing,' she said politely, and took him back to the palazzo. 'You're very welcome to use the sitting room or the library, if you need space to work.'

'Thanks, but it's fine,' he said, and shut himself away in his room.

Two days.

Serafina had two days left to make him fall in love with Venice and the palazzo.

Tonight, when the gondola had jolted her into his arms, she'd wondered. Surely the sunset and the gorgeous music and the stunning views would do it?

But she'd seen the precise moment he'd shuttered his feelings away.

Clearly someone had hurt him. Badly. Though she could hardly ask him what had happened. It was none of her business and nothing to do with working on the palazzo.

Plus her own attempts at compartmentalising her feelings weren't working. The more time she spent with him, the more she liked him. The more attractive she found him. The more she wanted to take a risk with him.

And to think this had all started with her idea of offering him a marriage of convenience. She knew now that definitely wasn't going to work. But was there a way of them seeing how things went between them, without either of them getting hurt?

The following morning, she took him to Murano to see glass being blown, and to take a photo of him for his mother. In the shop, he bought a stunning bowl for his sister and a vase for his mother. 'I can't resist this,' he said, picking up a starfish-shaped necklace in shades of teal and aqua. 'Sofia will love it, along with her gondolier teddy and her mask.'

'The glass here is pretty amazing,' she said. 'And some of the furnaces date back to medieval times.'

Once they'd had a look round the museum, she took him to the Basilica of St Mary and St Donatus. 'You have to see the dragon bones,' she said.

'Dragon bones?' he repeated, raising an eyebrow.

'The story goes back to the twelfth century. St Donatus slew a dragon who'd poisoned a well, and allegedly these are the bones of the dragon. One of the doges stole them and brought them here. They're probably the ribs of a whale,' she admitted with a smile, 'but it's a nice story. Plus the mosaic pavement here is gorgeous.'

He spotted the peacocks. 'Your favourites.'

She nodded, pleased that he'd remembered.

They wandered along the canal and cut through to a courtyard that opened up to a little square containing the most enormous glass star, in shades of blue and green and white.

'That's stunning,' he said.

'The Cometa di Vetro,' she said. 'Better still, it lights up at night. Another photo for your mother, I think.' This time, she took it on her phone. And she couldn't resist taking a close-up of him, too. Although the glass sculpture was beautiful, it was the man in front of them who took her breath away. And just for a moment she wished they were both tourists, enjoying the views and wandering around hand in hand, completely carefree.

She'd gone back into super-bright tour guide mode, Gianni thought. And he wanted the woman back. The woman who'd shown him so much over the last few days and was hiding herself again.

'It's a pity we don't have enough time to go to Burano today,' she said. 'The houses are painted all different colours: some are incredibly bright, so the canal side looks like a rainbow, and others are ice-cream shades. It looks so pretty, reflecting in the water.'

But nothing like as pretty as the woman walking by his side in a summery dress, a floppy hat and a smile that made his heart feel as if it had done a backflip, Gianni thought.

His hand brushed against hers as they walked along, and his skin tingled at the contact. The second time it happened, he couldn't resist entwining his fingers with hers. When she didn't pull away, it made him feel weirdly settled. As if he'd been looking for something for so long, and he'd finally found it.

He sneaked a glance at her, but her expression was unreadable.

It was complicated. He still didn't have a clue where this thing between them was going. But for now he wanted to just *be* and not think about anything other than walking hand in hand with a woman he really liked.

And maybe it was the same for her because, although she didn't comment on the fact that they were holding hands, her fingers tightened slightly round his.

He had to drop her hand when they came across a tour group and needed to squeeze by; but then the moment was broken and it felt too awkward to take her hand again. Particularly when she glanced at her watch and said, 'We need to get back to pick up the ladder.'

'Of course,' he said.

Back to business.

Which was sensible.

'Last bit,' he said when they got back to the palazzo with the ladder.

'Do you want me to come and hold a torch for you?' she asked.

'If you have time, that'd be good,' he said.

It turned out that there was a leak in the roof, which was why two of the rooms had been affected by damp. 'Again, it's fixable,' he said. 'And the good news is that most of the roof structure is sound, with the exception of the cracked tiles that let in the water, and some of the wood underneath it.' But he documented everything thoroughly, taking measurements and photographs.

And then, to stop himself doing something stupid—like kissing her—he shut himself away again to work on his report, while she cooked dinner.

They ate on the balcony, and Serafina kept the conversation light and easy, though inwardly she felt nothing of the kind. Today in Murano, when she and Gianni had held hands, she'd felt as if he really was falling in love with her city. And she thought that he understood how she felt about the palazzo: but she needed to be sure. She had one more day to make sure he'd completely fallen in love with Venice and the palazzo. And she'd already brought out all the big guns: the Palazzo Ducale, Ca d'Oro, St Mark's in the evening, the view of the sunset over the Grand Canal, the glassblowing.

She was running out of time.

So was the museum.

The next day, she took him to a quieter part of the city to see Tintoretto's house and told him about Tintoretto's daughter having to dress as a boy to do her artist's training. 'Women weren't allowed to do figure work because it meant drawing from nudes,' she explained. 'Gradually it changed, so aristocratic women and nuns could work on illustrated manuscripts or needlework. And eventually women could paint people. It's important to tell their stories.'

'You really love your job, don't you?' he asked softly.

'I love my job, I love my city, and I love my palazzo,' she said. 'Not necessarily in that order. They're all kind of mixed up together.' Which was why the restoration was so important to her.

'You still haven't taken me to see your museum,' he said.

Because she worried there was too much at

stake. What if his dislike of modern art put him off the idea of helping her? 'There's a lot of modern art you wouldn't enjoy,' she prevaricated. 'And I want you to see the bits of Venice I think you'll enjoy most. Come and see the Three Moors and their camel.' She distracted him with tales of the three statues and Sior Antonio Rioba with his metal nose, then took him down another little alley to show him an archway she thought he'd like.

But the grey skies had been darkening all morning, and raindrops started to spatter round them. What began as a light shower soon turned into something much heavier, and she took his hand. 'This way. I know where we can get some shelter.'

Gianni ran through the little *calle* with Serafina, and they ended up ducking through an archway into a *sotoportego*—one of the tunnels that went underneath a building and connected two streets.

Either everyone else had found shelter elsewhere, or they'd stayed indoors rather than venturing out when the rain started, because the *sotoportego* was deserted. He could hear the rain pattering down on the cobbles of the street; the air felt warm and damp.

He was still holding Serafina's hand. Just like he had in Murano—except it felt as if there was some electrical charge surrounding them, and all of a sudden he could hardly breathe. He was incredibly aware of her. The colour of her eyes. The curve of her mouth. Her scent. The feel of her skin against his.

She swayed towards him, and he was lost. He wrapped his free arm round her and drew her closer. The next thing he knew, he was kissing her. Their arms were wrapped tightly round each other; she was so close that he could feel her heart beating against his, and he was sure that she could feel the drumming of his own heart.

Time felt as if it had stopped. He couldn't even hear the rain any more, beating away time with every droplet. There was only the here and now. The warmth of her body against his. The way her mouth moved against his, offering and taking at the same time.

When he broke the kiss, he felt dizzy. Serafina's eyes looked huge in the shadows; her mouth was slightly swollen and reddened, and his own felt in the same state.

She breathed his name, and he tucked a loose tendril of hair behind her ear. Then somehow the pad of his thumb seemed to have a life of its own and it was tracing her jawline, her lower lip. Her mouth parted, and he desperately wanted to kiss her again.

'Serafina. I want you,' he whispered.

'I want you, too,' she whispered back. 'The palazzo's three minutes away from here at a run.'

Where he could kiss her in private, for as long as they both wanted, and they wouldn't have to stop.

The rain was drumming down hard again, almost in time with his heart.

He took her hand. 'Let's go.'

They ran through the rain together, neither of them caring that they were getting soaked.

And then they were at the back door of the palazzo, the street entrance. She opened the door; the second it closed behind them, they were kissing again.

He swept her up in his arms and carried her up the stairs. Her arms were wrapped round his neck and both of them were laughing; and he kissed her on every step up to the first floor, heedless of her disapproving ancestors looking down from the walls.

He carried her along the corridor to his bedroom, still kissing her; then finally set her down on her feet when he was standing next to his bed.

'Gianni.' She stroked her face, and his heart felt as if it had done a somersault. He'd never wanted anyone so much in his life.

'Are you sure about this?' he asked softly.

She answered him with a kiss that started out sweet and ended up scorching.

He'd been drawn to her since the moment they'd met. He'd wanted her since he'd danced in St Mark's Square with her. Since he'd held hands with her on Murano. And he couldn't resist her any more.

CHAPTER SEVEN

GIANNI LETO WAS the first man Serafina had made
love with since Tom. The first man she'd kissed
since Tom. The first man she'd really *noticed*
since Tom.

Apart from their initial meeting in Rome,
they'd barely known each other a week.

And yet she felt more in tune with him than
she had with the man who'd asked her to marry
him and then broken her heart.

The first time she and Gianni had made love,
it had been frantic, because they'd both needed
to slake their thirst for each other.

Then he'd taken time to explore her. He'd taken
her breath away, and she'd had the pleasure of
watching him come apart under her touch, too.

And now she was lying in Gianni's arms, her
head against his shoulder and her arm wrapped
round his waist, holding him close. Right then,
she was warm and comfortable and drowsy, and
she wanted to stay here for ever.

He dropped a kiss on top of her head. 'What

now?' he asked, his voice soft, but the words were enough to break the spell in her head.

'I don't know,' she said.

'You live in Venice. I live in Rome. Long-distance rela—' He stopped, and his arms tightened round her. 'Sorry. I know you've already been there and worn the T-shirt.'

Serafina and Tom hadn't even lived in the same continent, let alone the same country or the same city. She agreed with Gianni that long-distance relationships didn't work. Then again, relationships didn't work for her family, full stop. Plus he'd said that he was focusing on his business. She needed to focus on fixing the palazzo.

This thing between them didn't stand a chance: but she didn't want him to say it first. She didn't want to let herself get hurt again. Which left her with no choice but to say, 'I'm not looking for a relationship. I don't have the space in my life.' It wasn't completely true, but maybe if she told herself often enough she might start to believe it.

'Same here,' he said.

'What just happened…' She leaned her forehead against him for a moment. 'I think it was us getting something out of our systems. And now we need to go back to how things were. A business relationship.'

'Contractor and client,' he agreed.

Because even friendship wouldn't be enough.

Not now they'd made love. Not now she knew how he could make her feel.

And, much as she wanted to stay exactly where she was, she knew it would be a mistake and she'd end up eating her heart out for something she couldn't have. Better to leave now. While she could still pretend to be cool and calm and every centimetre a *contessa*. 'You have a report to finish writing,' she said, 'and I'm supposed to be working on an exhibition catalogue. Maybe we ought to…um…get up and do some work.' Which would buy her time to regroup and get her head back into sensible mode. 'Maybe we can talk again in a couple of hours.' She glanced at her watch. 'Over dinner. I'll buy you that lobster you wanted, in a posh restaurant.' It would wipe out her finances for the rest of the month, but she'd stopped caring.

'OK,' he said. 'But the lobster's on me.'

'My idea, my bill,' she corrected. 'Would you mind…um…closing your eyes?'

He smiled. 'Shy, considering what we just did?'

'I know. But I'm not brave, Gianni. I can't get up and saunter out of your room, naked.' Even if, strictly speaking, the room belonged to her and there was nobody else in the palazzo to see them. 'That's not who I am.'

He nodded. 'OK. Eyes closed. I'll open them again when I hear the door shut.'

She knew he meant it. Gianni Leto didn't say things he didn't mean. Unlike Tom, he was straightforward and honest. 'Thank you. Help yourself to whatever you want from the kitchen.' As soon as his eyes were closed, she slid out of bed, wrapped her clothes round her, and bolted.

Gianni kept his eyes closed even after the door had shut.

By sleeping together, he and Serafina had made everything much more complicated.

The problem was, now they'd spent an afternoon in bed together, it wasn't enough for him. He wanted more from her. He wanted everything.

But he knew he couldn't have it. How could he and Serafina have a future? They'd both agreed that long-distance relationships didn't work. No way would she move from Venice, away from the job she loved and the house she loved; and he didn't want to move from Rome, hours away from his family. There wasn't a middle ground.

Even if they could find a way round that, there were all the other barriers. They were from different worlds. Serafina had gold-framed portraits in a line up the staircase to illustrate her family tree; Gianni knew his ancestors back to his great-grandparents, and that was it. He was wealthy now, but his family was firmly rooted in a lower class than hers. Although he didn't think she was like Elena's family, he still had their words in their head, saying he wasn't good enough for them: and if he hadn't been good enough for them, how could he possibly think he was good enough for the family of a *contessa*? Money didn't change a thing.

Plus she'd explicitly said she didn't want a relationship; there was no point in trying to find a way to make it work.

From now on, he and Serafina were strictly business.

He wanted for long enough to make sure he wouldn't bump into her in the corridor, then took a shower before settling down with his laptop to finalise his report.

Serafina deleted the paragraph for the third time.

'For pity's sake, just *focus*,' she told herself crossly.

Daydreaming over Gianni Leto wasn't going to solve anything.

Making love with him had been a mistake. Instead of getting him out of her head, it had only succeeded in making her think about him even more.

How stupid this was. If he'd wanted her, he would've argued with her when she'd suggested taking their relationship back to a purely professional one. He hadn't. Obviously for him this had been getting it out of his system—and for him it had worked.

He didn't feel the same way she did.

And she didn't have time to brood about it. Right now she needed to sort out her work and sort out her finances, to get the palazzo fixed.

Though, given that Gianni had said he wasn't looking for a relationship, would he agree to her idea of a marriage of convenience? Only for a year?

She was still thinking about it when her phone shrilled. She glanced at the screen: her mother. No doubt she was double-checking the arrangements for her return home on Sunday. For the fourth time.

Forcing herself to sound a lot brighter than she actually felt, she answered the phone. 'Hello, Mamma. How are you?'

'I… Oh, Serafina.' Francesca burst into tears. 'I'm so sorry.'

'Mamma? What's wrong?' Dread flooded through her. Oh, no. Please don't let anything have happened to Tia Vittoria.

'I know I'm supposed to come back on Sunday afternoon, but I can't bear the idea of coming back to that house. All the damp and the lumpy beds and the shabbiness. It's a *tomb*.' Francesca sobbed again. 'I hate Venice. I *hate* that house. Without that place round our necks, maybe your father and I would have been happy. I know you're trying to fix things, but I don't think anyone can fix things where that place is concerned. And I can't live there any more. I just *can't*.'

Relief that Vittoria was all right was quickly replaced by dismay. If her mother wanted to move from the palazzo, then she would need somewhere to live. She'd also need an income. How on earth was Serafina going to find enough money to support two households—particularly as the palazzo was going to eat up every penny she had and then some?

Why, why, *why* hadn't her father been sensible enough to get his financial affairs in order and sort out a pension, to make sure Francesca had enough to live on if he died first? Why hadn't her mother nagged him into it, back in the days before his gambling addiction had taken such a hold? Why hadn't she realised that her parents were completely hopeless when it came to money, and acted sooner?

What was she going to do?

'Serafina?'

The last thing Serafina needed now was an outpouring of doom and gloom. 'I'm here, Mamma. Sorry. I was thinking something through.' Panicking, but her mother didn't need to know that.

'I know we can't afford it, but I just…' Francesca's voice hitched.

'Mamma—it's OK. I know Venice has a lot of unhappy memories for you.' Serafina took a deep breath. 'Don't worry about the money.' That was her job. It was always going to be her job, but it felt as if someone had piled yet another weight on her shoulders. The lightness of spirit she'd felt in Gianni's arms had vanished, replaced by dread. 'We'll find you somewhere nice, some-where near Tia Vittoria if that's what you'd like, and I'll make sure the bills are paid and you have enough money for a comfortable life.' She'd do it, even if she had to work three jobs and exist on less than four hours sleep a night.

'I'm sorry. I know I'm letting you down, leav-ing you all alone,' Francesca said.

'You're not letting me down at all, Mamma,' Serafina lied. 'I take it you're staying with Tia Vittoria for a bit longer?'

'Yes.'

At least she had a breathing space before she had to start paying rent. The tension in her shoul-ders eased a tiny bit. 'Do you need me to bring you anything from here? Or can it wait a few more days while—' she scrabbled frantically for a plausible excuse '—while I sort something out at the museum?'

'A few more days is fine. Vittoria and I are going shopping tomorrow.'

If Francesca put whatever she bought on credit,

that would give Serafina a few more days to work out how to find the money to pay for it. She'd have a quiet word with her aunt later to fill her in on the situation. 'That's good. Have a lovely time, Mamma. Sorry to be rude, but I need to go. Love you.'

When she ended the call, she stared at the table, unseeing.

Somehow, she had to find a way to pay for the restoration of the ground floor of the palazzo— and have the work done in the next three months so she could save the museum. And on top of that she needed to find her mother a house where she'd be comfortable but the finances were manageable.

The bank had refused her a loan, but Serafina knew that going to a loan shark for money wasn't the answer. Interest rates meant that the debt would spiral quickly.

Walking away wasn't an option. If she let the palazzo rot, then whoever inherited it would have the burden dumped on them—whether that was a distant cousin or her own child. That wasn't fair. It wasn't fair to the house, either.

She had to do something. Find someone who was willing to lend her money until the palazzo was back on its feet and the museum was safe.

But her brain felt completely empty. She didn't have a clue where she could go from here.

Right at that moment, she'd never felt more

alone, and a wave of hopelessness swamped her. Giving in to it, she put her face in her hands and sobbed.

As Gianni walked through the hallway to the kitchen to make himself a coffee, he could hear someone crying.

Big, hiccupping sobs.

It sounded as if Serafina was breaking her heart.

Even though they'd agreed to keep things strictly professional between them, he couldn't pretend he hadn't heard her crying. Though he also wasn't going to walk unannounced into her study. Not without a prop.

He made coffee and raided the cupboard for biscuits, put the lot on a tray, then rapped on the door of her study. 'Serafina?'

'Sorry, I'm a bit busy,' she called back.

No, she wasn't. And he'd despise himself if he walked away, knowing that she was upset. 'I heard you crying,' he said. 'I thought you could do with coffee and biscuits. I'm coming in.'

When he opened the door, she looked away from him and rubbed at her face; but when she turned back she couldn't disguise the puffiness of her eyes.

Something was obviously very, very wrong.

He wasn't conceited enough to think it was

because they'd called a halt to what was happening between them. It was more likely to do with the palazzo.

'Here. You don't have to talk. Not yet, anyway. Just eat one of these.'

She gave him a watery smile. 'Thank you. That's kind.'

He set the tray on her desk and sat in one of the armchairs—which turned out to be even less comfortable than it looked.

When it was finally obvious to him that she wasn't going to talk without a prompt, he said gently, 'Sometimes, it helps to talk to someone who's not involved.' He knew that wasn't strictly true of their situation; part of him *was* involved since he'd met her and come to Venice.

She looked at him, as if weighing up whether she could trust him. 'This stays between you and me?'

'It stays between you and me. I promise. And I don't break my promises,' he reassured her.

Her continued silence told her that either she didn't quite trust him, or that someone had let her down badly in the past.

But she'd trusted him with herself—something that he thought was more precious than whatever was holding her back right now.

He was about to break the silence when she took a deep breath. 'OK. Thank you.' She scrubbed at her face again. 'I don't even know where to start.'

'The beginning?' he suggested.

She gave him a very wan smile. 'I'm not quite sure where the beginning is.'

'Then start wherever you like,' he said.

'The palazzo, I guess.' She blew out a breath. 'Way, way back, my family were merchants. They did well for themselves. One of them married into the nobility and ended up with the palazzo—and then they found they had a status to maintain. They liked to entertain. And over the years the trade and the money dried up. Things were sold to pay for entertaining, instead of the money being used to fix problems with the house. I had no idea how bad it was until...' She swallowed hard. 'Until my dad died.'

'Yeah. I know how that feels. It changes everything,' he said. 'And you always look back and wonder if you could've done something to stop that heart attack happening, even though the sensible bit of you knows you couldn't and it was never your fault in the first place.'

She bit her lip. 'Sorry. I didn't mean to bring back bad memories for you.'

'It's fine,' he said. 'What I meant is that I probably understand more than someone who hadn't lost their dad to a heart attack.'

'Did your dad make mistakes?' she asked.

'The citizens of Bardicello would say so. Their town hall was a pretty big one,' he said. 'We were lucky nobody was hurt.' He looked at her. 'What was your dad's mistake?'

'He knew the house needed work and we didn't have the money to fix it.' She took a deep breath. 'He'd always enjoyed playing cards—and he'd always won.'

Lucky at cards, unlucky in love. The phrase slid into Gianni's head from out of nowhere.

'What I didn't know was that he didn't only play cards with his friends for relatively low stakes over a bottle of grappa, for fun. He played online. With a high credit limit, one he kept increasing. He had a few wins that encouraged him—but then he hit a losing streak.' She shook her head. 'He kept telling himself he'd get his lucky break and win it all back, and more. And he kept going.'

Then she stopped, as if she couldn't bear to go on.

'But the lucky break never came?' Gianni asked softly.

'It was a spiral. The more he lost, the more he gambled in an attempt to win it back, and the more he lost. That last loss was the really big one, the one that brought on the heart attack. And I didn't even know he was gambling like that. I was his daughter, I was living here, and I didn't know how bad things were. How could I have been that oblivious?'

'Addicts tend to be good at hiding things,' he said. 'Did your mum know?'

'To some extent, yes, but neither of us knew how bad it was until I started sorting out the estate. I still owe some of the inheritance tax, and I can't even use the art on the walls to pay it off because everything that *might* have been worth something is actually a copy. That's why the house will have to pay its way.' She looked away. 'Yeah, I know. Poor little rich girl. Doesn't your heart bleed for me?'

The savagery in her voice made him wince. 'Poor little rich girl? That's not who you are, Serafina. You're not expecting other people to bail you out,' he said. 'You're trying to sort out the problems yourself.'

'Even so. My mother hates this house. She says it's like a tomb.'

Her mother had a point, he thought. The palazzo did feel like a mausoleum.

'I promised to fix it and make things better… and I haven't even managed to start it. I've let her down. And she called me just now to say she doesn't want to come back to Venice. She wants to stay near Verona, where she grew up. Near her sister.'

And did Serafina's mother have an income?

Or would Serafina need to support her mother, too? he wondered.

'And I've let the museum down,' she continued.

'The museum you work for? Is that the one you wanted to have the ground floor?'

She nodded. 'I'm sorry. I should've been more open with you about that, but it isn't really my place to discuss it because I'm not the director.' She blew out a breath. 'Will you promise me this goes no further than you?'

'I promise,' he said.

'The lease on our building is up for renewal. Beppe, the guy who owns our building, wants to quadruple the cost of the lease.'

Gianni frowned. 'Surely that's illegal?'

'It ought to be,' she said, 'but Madi—the museum director—got a lawyer friend to look at it. It seems Beppe can do whatever he likes. There weren't any clauses protecting our lease when he bought the building. Either we have to increase our running costs hugely, which isn't an option, or we have three months to move the museum somewhere else with an affordable rent. The ground floor of the palazzo would be the perfect place. Except it needs bringing up to all the safety standards, first. The museum can't afford to pay for the renovations to the space, and I can't afford it, either.' She closed her eyes. 'I've let everyone down. We can loan the exhibits to other museums; at least they'll be stored in the right conditions. But it means the collection's going to be scattered after years and years of building it up.'

'It's not your fault, Serafina. You can't blame yourself for the business decision of someone who—'

'—wants to gut the building and turn it into an upmarket hotel,' she finished, her lip curling.

'I can see now,' he said dryly, 'why you looked so angry in Rome when I suggested selling your palazzo to a developer.'

She nodded. 'Developers aren't my favourite people. Though, even without the entailment, I wouldn't have sold the palazzo. But now I'm in a place where, however I look at it, I've let my mother down, I've let the museum down, and I've let the palazzo down. The only thing that I can think of that might work…' She shook her head. 'No. I can't ask you.'

Was she going to ask him for a loan, perhaps? Maybe he could help her. 'Try me,' he said.

She looked at him, her dark eyes luminous. 'Marry me?'

'What?' It was the last thing he'd expected. He couldn't see how marrying her would have anything to do with the restoration or her financial problems.

'I mean a marriage of convenience,' she clarified.

He still didn't get it.

When he said nothing, she said, 'We're both

single. There aren't any complications for either of us. We stay married for a year. You'll get the social cachet of my name and good publicity for your business, and I'll get the funds to start the restoration of the palazzo.'

'How exactly does marrying me get you funds? Or are you straight out saying that you want to marry me for my money?' he drawled, trying to disguise the sting of hurt. Even Elena's family hadn't been that bold.

'It's not *your* money I want,' she said. 'It's the magazine's.'

'What magazine?'

'*Celebrity Life*. If we give them an exclusive on our wedding photos, they'll pay us a fee. Enough to make a start on the renovations.'

Gianni could hardly believe he was hearing this.

He wasn't sure what annoyed him most: the idea of marrying for money, the way she'd talked about giving him social cachet, or the fact she could come out with this outlandish proposal when they'd just spent the afternoon in bed together *and* they'd both said they weren't looking for a relationship.

'No,' he said.

She spread her hands. 'See? I told you I couldn't ask you.'

'Where did you get that ridiculous idea from in the first place?'

She looked away. 'It was the deal I had when Tom… Well. It doesn't matter, because the wedding didn't happen.'

Gianni had always thought himself a reasonable judge of character, but he'd failed with Elena—and, worse, it seemed he hadn't learned from that and he'd made exactly the same mistake with Serafina. It made him feel sick to discover that she was as much of a snob with her eye on the money as Elena had been, deep down. Anger bubbled through him and he couldn't help lashing out. 'I'm not surprised he changed his mind about marrying you, if you'd set up a deal like that.'

She flinched. 'It wasn't *my* deal. It was Tom's publicist's. I'd planned to donate my half of the money to a good cause.'

'Like fixing up your palazzo?'

'No, actually. I was going to give it to a women's refuge. One that had helped a friend.' She narrowed her eyes at him. 'And, for your information, Tom wasn't the one who called off the wedding. I was.'

Now he felt guilty. Maybe he'd got her wrong, after all.

But he couldn't quite apologise, not when she'd asked him to marry her for money.

He'd grown up knowing what a good marriage was. Yes, his family had been poor, but his parents had loved each other and they'd loved their children. No way was he settling for anything less. Marriage might be a business deal for a countess, but it wasn't that for him. 'Marriage should be for love.'

'I don't believe in love,' she said. 'It's a fairy tale.'

He couldn't help sniping. 'And you're Cinderella, are you, Contessa?'

'No. I simply have a bit of a cash flow problem.' She sighed and raked her hand through her hair. 'I didn't intend to insult you, Gianni. But I was trying to think of how I could raise the money to start restoring the palazzo. The magazine had offered us money for the wedding photos. Tom, being the Hollywood star, was the obvious draw; but I had a quiet word with the magazine and it seems their readers like—well, royal stuff.'

At least she squirmed when she said it. Not that it was much consolation to him.

'And it seems a Venetian *contessa* counts as "royal stuff". They offered me a deal. Obviously not as much money as they would've paid if I'd still been marrying a movie star, but enough to fund the first bit of the restoration. And then I'd have the rent coming in from the museum—even though I'd rather them not have to pay me any rent at all—and that would pay for renovating the top two floors to rent out as accommodation. At a fair rent. And then the money coming in from the accommodation would pay for renovating my floor, and once that was all done I could drop the museum's rent to a peppercorn.'

She was putting herself last again, he noticed. And he could see the logic behind her reasoning, even if he didn't approve of it. 'A marriage of convenience is a bad idea,' he said. 'I believe in marrying for love, the way my parents did.'

She looked away. 'Love doesn't work where my family is concerned.'

'Why not?'

'Because of the curse.'

This was the first he'd heard of it. 'What curse?'

'Remember I showed you Marianna's portrait?' As his nod, she continued, 'When Marianna died, her lover cursed our family and said that no Ardizzone would ever have a happy marriage. Yes, I know that all sounds completely ridiculous and melodramatic: but, if I look at my family history, there's a long line of unhappy marriages. My grandparents loathed each other. My parents weren't happy—when I look at it now, I realise my dad's gambling made my mum more anxious, and the more doom-and-gloom she got the more he turned to gambling, and it was a vicious spiral. And I'm pretty sure it's been like that for all the generations before them.'

'What about you?'

Her eyes were bleak. 'I thought I was the one

who'd break the curse. I met Tom at a glitzy party when he made a movie here—our museum was the venue—and we hit it off instantly. He asked me out, and pretty much swept me off my feet. I honestly thought he was The One. When he asked me to marry him, I said yes. But then I flew out to LA a couple of weeks later to surprise him.' Her eyes darkened. 'When I let myself in to his flat, I found him in bed with someone else.'

He knew she'd been engaged, but he'd had no idea that the guy had cheated on her.

Before Gianni could even process that, Serafina continued, 'It turned out she wasn't even the first. He'd been cheating on me even before he asked me to marry him. The curse of the Ardizzones held true.' She blew out a breath. 'If you don't marry for love, then you don't have unrealistic expectations and it's not going to go wrong.'

He thought about it.

But Elena hadn't really loved him. Not enough to stand by him when things became difficult after the building collapse at Bardicello: she'd broken off their engagement within days. Maybe he'd had unrealistic expectations; but he thought that the lack of love was what would have wrecked their marriage if they'd actually got that far.

'My parents married for love,' he said. 'And they still loved each other on the day my dad died.'

'Maybe they were just lucky,' she said.

'My sister and her husband love each other, too,' he said. 'So, no. I don't think my parents were lucky. They worked at it.'

Her eyes narrowed. 'Are you saying that my family gave up on their marriages? That they used the curse as an excuse?'

'It's one possibility,' he said. 'And I think that's a more likely explanation than a curse.'

At that, all the fight went out of her. 'Probably,' she said. 'Though, curse or no curse, it doesn't change my situation now. Even if you agreed to let me make stage payments, I'd still need the money from the magazine to pay for the first lot of renovations until the ground floor was properly useable and the rent from the museum came onstream.'

'Was that the plan when you contacted me? I was single, so you thought you could ask me to marry you, have my picture plastered all over a celeb magazine and then take the money?'

'Yes. No. I mean, I did think it, at first,' she admitted. 'But my best friend said it was a stupid idea. My aunt did, too. I came to see you because I thought you'd do a good job—and because I thought you might know more than I do on the building side of things and could advise me who to contract to try and get a grant. I know the system from a heritage point of view, for exhibits, but not for the buildings.'

He was still digesting this. 'You were going to ask me to marry you—before you'd even *met* me? Is that why you asked me to spend a week here?'

'No. I wanted you to see the place for yourself and do an honest assessment,' she said. 'And in return I was offering you a week's accommodation in an amazing location. A *quid pro quo*. Though I admit, I hoped that when I showed you Venice—*my* Venice, full of buildings and art and lovely things—you'd fall in love with city and see the potential of the palazzo, and that would persuade you to help me. And then maybe I could ask you about the—well, the magazine.'

Had she wanted him to fall in love with her, as well as with the city and the palazzo? Because he knew he was close to it. Crazily close.

Was that why she'd slept with him? Because she was using him, the same way Elena had?

Or did Serafina feel that same pull of attraction that he did, but she wouldn't let herself believe in it because all her forebears had been married unhappily and her own engagement had ended in misery?

Maybe it was a mixture of the two.

But, the more he thought about it, the more Gianni felt that it had been a set-up, all along.

To a point, her plan had worked. He'd fallen in love with Venice. He wanted to work on the palazzo and bring it back to life. And he was more than halfway to falling in love with Serafina.

But it was still a set-up, and that was more than he could stomach. 'A marriage of convenience.' Even Elena hadn't offered him that. Or had she, but she hadn't spelled it out the way Serafina had?

'I'm sorry,' Serafina said. 'It wasn't meant as an insult. And I know it's a stupid idea. Born out of despera—' She stopped. 'Sorry. I'm digging myself a deeper hole. And you've been so nice.'

'Nice' wasn't how he was feeling right now. At all. 'Two years ago,' he said, 'I was engaged.'

She looked at him.

'Elena was from...not the aristocracy, like you, but from "a good family".' He punctuated it with air quotes. 'One who wasn't happy that she was marrying a man whose father worked his way up from nothing, in a trade. But having money kind of made up for my lack of social respectability.'

She narrowed her eyes at him. 'That's appalling snobbery.'

'But weren't you just offering me the same? Your name, to make me respectable?' Which made her as bad as Elena, in his view.

She was silent for a moment, clearly thinking about what she'd said. 'Respectable in the eyes of people who were judging you unfairly. It never occurred to me how insulting that was, and I apologise.'

He could see that she meant it. 'Apology accepted,' he said.

'The way I saw it, I was trying to see what I could offer you in return for your help. Good publicity and the Ardizzone name seemed a reasonable way of doing it. I honestly didn't intend to make you feel as if you were…' She shook her head. 'You're not beneath *anyone*, Gianni. You're the CEO of a construction company—yes, it was your father's company, but you worked your way up right from when you were small and helped him mix mortar on a Saturday morning. And you studied for your degree at the same time as putting in a full day's work. There aren't many people who could do that. You deserve recognition for what you've achieved, not dismissiveness.'

Her eyes were full of fire, and he realised with shock that it was all for him.

'I apologise for being intrusive, but I don't understand. What happened to your engagement?' she asked.

'Bardicello,' he said with a shrug. 'Elena's family didn't want to be associated with it. They didn't want their name tainted with the scandal.'

She frowned. 'But if Elena loved you, why didn't she stand up to her family? Why didn't she stand beside you? None of it was your fault.'

Because he hadn't been enough for Elena. She hadn't wanted to fight for him. Rather than say that, he focused on what else Serafina had said. 'I thought you didn't believe in love?'

'For me, I don't. But for other people…' She spread her hands.

In Elena's shoes, would Serafina have stood by him? He rather thought the answer was yes. This time he was honest, even though it hurt to say it. 'She didn't love me enough,' he said.

'I'm sorry. You deserved better.'

Said the woman who'd walked in on her ex being unfaithful to her, not long after they'd got engaged. 'So did you.' He looked her in the eye. 'But I still believe love exists.'

'For you, maybe. Not for my family.'

'Curses,' he said, 'are not real.'

'But families tend to follow patterns,' she said.

'That's true,' he acknowledged. 'But you're already breaking one pattern in your family. You're doing something about the palazzo instead of ignoring the problems and letting it decay further. Why not break the pattern of unhappy relationships, too?'

'I'm trying to do something about the palazzo, but I'm failing,' she said. 'What I have is a building that needs fixing before I can make it earn its keep, debts that are increasing daily, and I'm letting down my mother and I'm letting down the museum.' She shook her head. 'I can't see any way forward. I'm *stuck*.'

Not only with the palazzo, he thought, but with an unrealistic view of love. But he'd have to deal with one thing at a time. The palazzo was definitely easier to deal with than emotions were. 'And the bank won't lend you anything?'

'They were my first port of call.' She rolled her eyes at him. 'Obviously I didn't totter in, bat my eyelashes at them and ask them for money. I gave them a business plan. Before Madi told me about the museum's lease, originally I was going to resign from the museum and get a paid job to support my mother and pay the bills, and I'd offer holiday accommodation to tourists.' She spread her hands. 'The bank said no.'

'Hang on. Backtrack a second. The museum doesn't pay you?'

'Technically I'm a volunteer—not simply the board stuff, but the day-to-day work I do there as well,' she said. 'If you want to make lots of money, you don't work in the heritage sector. I thought I had family money to support me, and if the museum didn't pay me then it meant they could offer a paid position to someone who wanted to work in heritage but needed a salary.'

He noticed she'd said she'd *thought* she had family money. Clearly that wasn't the case.

'What happened to the family money?'

'We have a trust fund. My dad was the trustee. He moved some of the investments to beat the market, except the market beat him. And then he borrowed some of the funds to try and make the money back,' she said grimly. 'Mamma and I have been living on my savings for the last six months.'

'Your dad embezzled the trust fund?'

She frowned. 'No. He didn't *steal* it. He always intended to pay it back.'

Gianni was truly shocked. Then again, gambling was an addiction, and addicts didn't tend to have the clearest view of their actions.

Serafina's financial situation was worse than he'd guessed, though at least she'd finally been honest with him. She didn't have the money to begin the repairs, but she had a strong sense of responsibility—to her family and to the museum—and it was clear that she was trying to find a way to rescue everyone and everything.

He could walk away. Go back to Rome and pretend he'd never met her or seen this place.

Or he could act on his instincts. The voice in his heart that urged him to step in and help her, because she needed someone on her side—and he knew what that felt like, thanks to Bardicello and the way he'd had to struggle afterwards to persuade clients that their firm could still be trusted. He'd ended up keeping an online diary of the restoration, with video and photographs, and that had helped to restore their confidence. But for a while he'd felt very, very alone.

'So we have a little under three months to get the ground floor fixed,' he said.

She stared at him, hope lighting her expression. 'Does this mean you've changed your mind and you'll marry me?'

'No. I still don't believe in a marriage of convenience,' he said. 'If I ever marry, it'll be for love. I won't accept anything less—and neither should you. Patterns can be broken. You don't have to be defined by your parents, or your grandparents, or that long line of miserable portraits in your hallway. They're part of you, yes, but there's more to you than that.'

She inclined her head in acknowledgement. 'But how does that get my palazzo fixed? Do you know somewhere that will offer me a grant, or a loan?'

'Me,' he said quietly.

Her eyes widened. 'But I can't expect that from you. Not after…' She flushed. 'After the way I've treated you.'

'You love this house,' he said. 'You want to make it shine again. And you're trying to help the museum. You said that if you can get the ground floor fixed, the rent paid by the museum will pay for the upper floors to be repaired and converted to accommodation, and then renting those floors out will finance the repairs to your floor.'

He looked at her. 'Do you have the figures to back that up?'

'I do.' She got out of her chair and gestured to him to take a seat. 'Let me show you.'

She brushed against him as she switched out of the word processing program and into the spreadsheet. He could feel the warmth of her skin, smell the light floral perfume she wore, and suddenly it was a struggle to think straight, because he was sideswiped by the memories of making love with her.

'Gianni?'

He pulled himself together and looked at the figures she'd put together.

'I assume the rent the museum will be paying is the same as they're paying now?'

'Proportionally less, because the space is smaller. But it works,' she said.

'But they don't pay you a salary. Without an income you're going to be in trouble.'

'Madi says she's going to try and get me a salary. I don't need much,' she said. 'Enough to support my mother, wherever she decides to live, and cover my food and the basic bills for the palazzo. It'll be six months before I start needing to heat the place again, and the bills are a bit more manageable over the summer.'

Elena would've complained about not being able to buy new clothes and shoes, he thought. Serafina had completely ignored those aspects.

And she'd thought of her mother before anything else. His first instincts about her had been right, after all—even if she had made that stupid suggestion about a marriage of convenience.

'I know you have to pay some of the costs upfront—the materials and the labour—but if there's a way you can hold off for three months before I need to start paying you back, then I'll repay every single cent. With interest,' Serafina said. 'And I'm pretty sure everyone at the museum will muck in and help with the restoration in their spare time, including me.'

'Are any of them trained construction workers?' he asked.

'No, but not every single task in a restoration needs someone who's trained, does it? There's fetching and carrying, preparation work and painting walls—the kind of things people do when they redecorate their own homes,' she said. 'Or whatever your team directs us to do.'

'Extra help with that sort of thing will help to cut the time and the costs,' he said.

'When you do site visits, you're very welcome to stay here,' she said.

Site visits. What if he stayed and oversaw the restoration personally? Then he'd be working side by side with her every single day…

It was way, way too tempting.

And it would be much too easy to fall back into

bed with her. Fall all the way in love with her. End up torn between Venice and Rome.

'And any of your crew's welcome to stay here, too,' she said.

Because it would cut the costs of the project? Or because it meant they'd have other people in the palazzo to act as a buffer between them? Did she feel the same way that he did, this weird mixture of longing and need warring with a determination to be sensible?

'I'll probably hire in local people for the crew,' he said, 'but thank you for the offer.'

'And your mother and your sister are very welcome to stay, and—'

'I get it,' he cut in. 'Now, let me go and get my laptop and we'll go through the notes I've made about the building, so we can work out our business strategy.'

'OK.'

But then her stomach growled. 'Sorry. I guess I'm hungry.' She grimaced. 'Sorry again. I promised you lobster tonight.'

Lobster she couldn't afford, and he knew she was too proud to let him pay. Plus, given how upset she'd been, he guessed she wouldn't feel like going out. He'd let her keep her dignity. 'I'm not really in the mood for going out,' he said, and the relief in her face told him he'd made the right choice.

'I could order a pizza,' she suggested.

He raised an eyebrow. 'Remember where I come from.'

That made her smile. 'Yeah. I admit, the pizza in Venice isn't as good as Rome. But at least it's quick.'

'By the time it's been delivered, I could have cooked pasta, served up two bowls, and we could've eaten it,' he pointed out.

She blinked. 'You cook?'

'Have all the men in your life been that hopeless?' He shook his head. 'My mother would've shooed every single one of them into her kitchen and made them repeat the dish until they'd got it right.'

She smiled at that, and he knew he'd managed to ease some of the misery she felt.

'I assume you have pasta, cheese and eggs in your kitchen?'

'Yes,' she said.

'Then I'll make us carbonara, and we'll eat on your balcony. If you want to go and freshen up, we'll be eating in ten minutes.'

CHAPTER EIGHT

IT FELT STRANGE to have someone else taking charge—particularly here at the palazzo, Serafina thought. But at the same time it was wonderful to feel that not all the burdens of the world were entirely on her shoulders.

Why had she assumed that Gianni couldn't cook? He was the kind of man who could do absolutely anything he put his mind to.

And again she felt guilty for suggesting a marriage of convenience. Of course he'd want the real deal: something she couldn't give him. He must've thought her as much of a snob as his ex's family.

Well, she'd prove to him she wasn't like that.

She'd do whatever any of his team asked her to do at the palazzo during a working day, and then finish her museum work in the evenings.

In the bathroom mirror, she could see what a mess she looked, her eyes puffy and her cheeks tear-stained. But at least now she had hope. There wasn't that crushing feeling of being alone and not being able to hold everything up, any more.

She washed her face and tied her hair back, then headed for the kitchen. 'Can I do anything to help?'

'Nope.' Gianni, looking perfectly at ease in front of the stove, smiled. 'You have two minutes until it's cooked.'

'Right. I'll set the table, then,' she said, grabbing cutlery from the drawer. 'Wine?'

'Water for me, please,' he said, 'because after dinner we're working on figures.'

She filled a jug with water, picked up two glasses, and had just finished setting the table on the balcony when he bought out two steaming bowls of carbonara.

'This is really good,' she said after the first mouthful.

'Don't sound so surprised,' he said dryly.

'It wasn't meant to be insulting,' she said. 'I was trying to be appreciative. It's lovely not to be the one doing all the cooking. I assume from what you said earlier that your mum taught you?'

'She says everyone should be able to make some basic food. Even my dad could cook a good arrabbiata,' he said.

Serafina thought of her own father. He would never have dreamed of standing in front of a stove. Neither would her mother. They'd had a housekeeper until Serafina came back from Rome; when the housekeeper had retired, Serafina had stepped in to do the cooking on the days when her parents didn't eat out.

Maybe if they'd done more of the everyday things, life might've been a bit easier for them.

Not that it would make any difference now.

Gianni kept the conversation light until they'd finished eating. Then he fetched his laptop and went through his notes. The more he showed her, the worse it looked.

'Thank you for being thorough,' she said. 'Bottom line: can we fix the ground floor in three months, or not?'

'Everything's possible,' he said. 'My dad taught me that. There might have to be some compromises, but it's possible. I need to find a local workforce—but that's something I do in every job, because if local people are involved in a project they'll tend to support it.'

'Good point,' she said.

'If your colleagues at the museum can join the team to do some of the non-skilled jobs, as you suggested, that would be helpful.' He looked at her. 'Your director—I know it's super-short notice, but if she could meet us tonight or tomorrow, then we could go through what we need to do and make a proper project plan. Then I can go back to Rome tomorrow, sort out whatever I need to do there, and we'll start work next week. I'll oversee the restoration myself.'

'And the costs?'

'Your figures stack up,' he said. 'Once the museum's moved in here and they're paying rent, that can start to pay for the next stage of renovations.'

'But what about the costs of the first stage?'

'You asked for a three-month delay before you start paying, plus I can get Flora to look into grants. We'll work something out,' he said. 'I know you'll pay me back.'

'Thank you doesn't seem enough,' she said.

He shrugged. 'It's enough.'

'Though I want a proper contract drawn up to make it clear I'm paying you back. With interest at the current bank base rate plus one per cent.'

'I'll get a contract sorted out next week,' he said.

'I still can't believe you're doing this. Especially as you hardly know me, and I pretty much insulted you earlier.'

'Everyone deserves a second chance,' he said. 'My dad taught me that. And what goes around, comes around. Be kind, and when you need kindness someone will be kind to you. You're already trying to do something good for other people. Fixing problems that you've inherited. I think you could use a friend.'

The problem was, friendship wasn't what she wanted from Gianni Leto. Though, with that stupid marriage of convenience proposal, she'd ruined the chance of their relationship turning into anything else.

'I could indeed. To friendship,' she said, raising her glass of water.

'And to the success of the palazzo,' he said, chinking his glass against hers. 'Call your boss and see when she's free.'

Maddalena was free that evening; she came over and walked through the ground floor with them.

'The light's wonderful. You were right, Serafina. It's the perfect space for the museum,' she said.

'As it is, or do you want partitions put up to make smaller rooms and give you more display space?' Gianni asked.

'Partitions would be good. And a small space for a gift shop and a café,' Maddalena said. 'We'll also need bathrooms and wheelchair access.'

In Serafina's kitchen, they sat down and worked out exactly what they needed.

'I'll talk to an architect friend tonight,' Gianni said. 'He owes me a favour, so that's not going to be an additional cost. I'll give him your list and the measurements, and hopefully he can help us make this space work the way you need it but without making too many changes to the heritage.'

'We might be able to get a grant towards some of the costs,' Maddalena said, 'though you know how slowly administrative things work. Serafina, because you're charging us less rent than we're paying now—'

'Because the space is smaller—it's in proportion per square metre, and I'll make sure you have the figures to make it all transparent for the rest of the board,' Serafina cut in.

Maddalena gave a nod of acknowledgement. 'It means we can afford to change your position to a salaried one, from the first day we move here.'

And that in turn would mean that Serafina could afford to rent somewhere comfortable for her mother. 'Thank you,' she said.

Maddalena stayed for a glass of wine on the balcony; when Serafina saw her out, she said, 'I like him. He's one of the good guys—not to mention being gorgeous.'

Serafina felt a blush steal into her face.

'And it's obvious he likes you,' Maddalena said.

'We're friends. Or becoming friends,' Serafina amended.

'Think about it,' Maddalena advised. 'Not all gorgeous men are as self-absorbed and selfish as a certain actor we won't name. He'd be good for you—and he'd also be lucky to have you.'

'This isn't about anything other than the palazzo,' Serafina said.

'Hmm.' Maddalena gave her a hug.

'I like your boss,' Gianni said when Serafina came back to the balcony. 'She tells it like it is.'

Serafina nodded. 'Indeed.'

'I've spoken to Stefano—my architect friend. He's going to get us some preliminary drawings for Monday. Flora's going to look up grants and see what she can do. And I've changed my train ticket to first thing tomorrow.'

'You did all that while I was saying goodbye to Madi?' Serafina stared at him. 'Was I ages, or can you do six million things at once?'

'There's no point in waiting unnecessarily,' he said.

So it really was going to happen.

She realised she'd spoken aloud when he said, 'Yes. Team Ca' d'Ardizzone for the win.'

'It's been a horrible few months. I didn't think there was any hope on the other side,' she admitted.

'I've been there,' he said. 'With Bardicello. I know how it feels. We had customers cancelling on us all over the place, and I had to prove to them that we were reliable. I put a video diary of the restoration on our website, and that helped a lot. But for a while I thought we were going to lose Dad's business, and I wasn't doing enough to fix it.'

Impulsively, she reached across the table to squeeze his hand—then wished she hadn't when desire licked up her spine.

This afternoon wasn't to be repeated.

She was in Gianni's debt.

And, until she was out of it again and could meet him as his equal, she needed to keep things strictly business between them.

Back in Rome, Gianni got the grilling he expected from his sister.

'You've known her a week, you're fixing her palazzo and you're not even charging her?' Flora put her hands on her hips and glared at him. 'You had sex with her, didn't you?'

He winced. 'That makes it sound bad.'

'It *is* bad. And utterly crazy.'

'And not quite accurate,' he said. 'She's going to pay me every single cent of the renovation costs. I'm simply giving her staged payments. The first one will start in three months, when the museum starts paying rent.'

'What if she doesn't pay you back?'

'She will,' Gianni said. 'Apart from anything else, it'll be in our contract. At her insistence.'

'Poor little rich girl.' Flora shook her head. 'I don't like this, Gi. She sounds like another Elena.'

'No. She's nothing like Elena. Elena would've walked away from this and let someone else deal with the problems. Serafina's taking responsibility and sorting them out herself—even though she inherited the problems rather than creating them,' Gianni said. 'She says you're welcome to come and stay at any time—you, Rico, Sofia and Mamma.'

'I suppose at least she made you relax a bit and have fun, judging from those photos,' Flora said.

He remembered dancing with her. Kissing her in the rain. Making love with her.

Flora coughed. 'You're blushing, Gi.'

'No, I'm not.' Though his face felt hot.

'You're smitten. Which doesn't bode well for this job,' Flora said, narrowing her eyes. 'It's always a mistake to let emotions get in the way of your business judgement.'

'Flora, look at the facts. I'm going to work on a palazzo nobody's touched for decades—in part, maybe for centuries,' Gianni said. 'With structural challenges I studied at university but never had the chance to put into practice. It's a dream job.'

'You still haven't sold it to me. It might be a dream job, but in the real world it could be a nightmare.'

'Let me show you.' He opened his laptop and brought up the spreadsheet.

Flora read through it carefully. 'Everything I'd want to see is there. And it looks sensible,' she said at last. 'But I'm still going to double-check your figures before we draw up a contract. And I need you to promise me that you won't lift a finger on the place, hire a team or order any materials until that contract is signed.'

'Flora, we kind of have a ticking clock.' He explained the museum's situation.

'You just said "we", not "she",' Flora said gently. 'Be careful, Gi. It sounds as if your heart's involved more than your head. I don't want to see you hurt again, the way Elena hurt you.'

'Serafina won't hurt me.'

'I hope not.' Flora bit her lip. 'I worry about you.'

'I'm fine. You don't have to worry.' Gianni gave her a hug. 'But I appreciate you having my back.'

How could you miss someone after a single day? Serafina wondered. But she kept herself busy on the Sunday, packing things her mother wanted and taking them to Verona so she could spend the day with her mother and her aunt. Vittoria suggested that Francesca should stay with her for a couple more months before starting to look for a house; and Serafina was thrilled to see that her mother seemed a lot happier away from the palazzo.

'I feel guilty for abandoning you,' Francesca said.

'You haven't abandoned me, Mamma,' Serafina reassured her. 'I'm sorting the palazzo out. Once it's restored, you might feel differently about it. You'll always have a home there. But what I want most is to see you happy. Verona's not far from Venice. We can still see lots of each other.'

Though when she was back in the palazzo, that evening, it felt as if she was rattling round. There were too many echoes from the past.

But she was going to change things. Make Ca' d'Ardizzone a happy place again. With Gianni's help.

On Monday afternoon, Gianni sent Serafina an email with a contract for her to check with her lawyers, along with a schedule of works, saying that he'd be back in Venice on Thursday morning. She called her solicitor and arranged a meeting for them both to sign the contract with the solicitor as a witness on Thursday.

In the meantime, Serafina spent her days working in the museum, helping to sorting out the plan to pack and move the exhibits, and her evenings packing up as much as she could on the ground floor of the palazzo ready for the restoration to start.

On Thursday, she was awake ridiculously early, filled with adrenalin. Today she'd be seeing Gianni again. She'd managed to get into professional mode by the time she met him at the train station, although her heart felt as if it had done a backflip when she caught sight of him walking out of the station entrance.

'Good to see you,' he said, shaking her hand.

'You too,' she said, trying to suppress the urge to throw her arms round him and kiss him. He was clearly keeping a professional distance; she'd do the same.

They caught the *vaporetto* back to the palazzo to drop off his suitcase.

'You're in the same room as last time, if that's OK,' she said.

'That's great.'

'And you need somewhere to work. It's up to you whether you'd rather have the dining room or the study.'

'The dining room's fine,' he said. 'It'll save you having to move—plus it means I have a big table to spread out on.'

It was only then she realised she'd hoped that he'd suggest sharing her study.

Which was ridiculous.

He was here to do a job. Sharing a study would be too distracting.

'You've already done a lot of packing,' he said when she let them into the palazzo.

And cleaning; even though the building work would create a lot of mess, she wanted the place clean before they started. 'You can hardly start work if there's clutter everywhere. The boxes are all numbered, and I have a master list of what's in each one.'

He looked approving. 'I've interviewed people over video calls, and I was hoping to meet up with the people I want on the crew here tomorrow, if that works for you.'

'You're the project manager,' she said. 'You're in charge of arranging things.' She fished in her bag and brought out a door key. 'And you need this, so you don't have to worry about whether I'm here or at the museum.'

'Thank you. For the back door, I assume?' he checked.

'Yes. And I'm getting the key to the side water gate copied for you to give you access for deliveries.'

Once the contracts had been signed, time seemed to move at a rapid pace. The next thing Serafina knew, the ground floor was full of builders and electricians and plumbers; walls and floors were being stripped back to bare bones; the air was full of dust; and there was the sound of hammers and drills everywhere, mingled with people talking and laughing and radios playing.

How long had it been since there were this many people in the house?

It was noisy and messy. Her mother would've hated it. But she loved it. She enjoyed the way the builders all greeted her in the morning, the way they smiled at her when she brought them mugs of coffee and plates of biscuits, and their patience as they taught her new skills so she could be a part of the restoration, too.

Gianni was right in the middle of things, doing physical work as well as directing his team, and every time she glanced at him she was more and more aware of him. In faded jeans and a T-shirt that showed off his muscular shoulders to perfection, he was utterly gorgeous.

But she couldn't let herself act on that attraction. Not while she was in his debt for the palazzo restoration. She'd simply have to suppress the memories of dancing with him in the twilight, kissing him in the rain, and making love with him in the bedroom next to hers.

So she smiled, she worked hard, and she kept things as professional as she could.

Serafina was definitely keeping him at a distance. Gianni had thought that taking the palazzo out of the equation might make things easier between them, but it had actually made things more complicated. Now they had a formal business relationship, it had put another barrier between them. She was working ridiculously hard, too, disappearing into her library straight after dinner to keep up with her museum work as well as helping the renovation team during the day.

How was he going to persuade her to let him close?

He managed to distract himself by checking through the schedule and working out what needed to be done next, when Robi, the site manager, came over. 'Gi, we've found something a bit unusual by the water gate. I wanted to check it with you before we carry on.'

Gianni followed him over to the water gate; some of the team had been working on the jetty, taking out the damaged bricks and mortar work.

'From outside, we found a cupboard behind the wall,' Robi said, 'but there's no sign of it on the inside of the house. You can see it for yourself.' He indicated the spot. 'It's flat plasterwork.'

Gianni looked at it, frowning. 'That's where I had high damp readings inside. I assumed water had come in through the cracked mortar and damaged brickwork and soaked into the plaster. But, as there's a cupboard there, maybe the water came through the doorway and someone blocked it up.'

'Instead of sorting it out properly by replacing

the bricks and the mortar and making the outside waterproof.' Robi rolled his eyes. 'There's a space underneath the cupboard with a wrapped bundle. It looks old. We thought you ought to see it before we take it out.'

Gianni followed him out onto the jetty, took the proffered torch and checked the hollow space beneath the former cupboard. As Robi had described, there was a wrapped bundle. 'Good call, Robi.' He took his phone from his pocket and took a quick snap of the bundle, using a flash to get a better picture. 'I think Serafina needs to see this. I'll go and get her.'

'Come in,' Serafina called at the rap on the library door.

'Got a minute? The site manager's found something interesting,' Gianni said. 'Did you know there was a cupboard by the water gate—the merchants' gate, not the front one?'

She frowned. 'I've never seen one there.'

'We've been taking out the damaged bricks and mortar, and the team found the cupboard—from the outside. There's a space beneath the floorboards of the cupboard and there's a bundle of something beneath it.'

'Have you taken it out and opened it?'

He shook his head. 'I thought you ought to see it, first. I've taken a photograph.' He showed her on his phone. 'It looks to me as if someone put it there deliberately.'

Serafina took a pair of cotton gloves from her desk drawer. At his surprised glance, she explained, 'It might not be anything important—but, if it's a book or a diary, the gloves will at least protect it from the oils on my fingertips. Just in case it's something important, if I give you my camera, can you document it as we go?'

'Of course,' he said.

She followed him down to the water gate. 'There's no sign of a cupboard on this side of the wall.'

'From the outside, you can see that the door's this side,' he said. 'The opening's been plastered over. It could be that the cupboard was damp and it was shut off, so nobody made the mistake of storing anything in it.'

'That sounds about right, where my family's concerned,' she said grimly. 'Though my dad never mentioned a hidden cupboard. It must've been shut off for at least sixty years.'

She peered into the recess from the jetty.

'Can you reach it?' Gianni asked.

'Just about.'

'OK. Stop there while I take a picture—and now I'm switching to my phone to film you.'

She brought the bundle out into the light.

'It's about the right size, weight and shape for a

book. It looks as if it's been wrapped in leather,' she said. 'Maybe to try and keep the contents waterproof. If it's a diary, that would make sense. Let's go and take a proper look inside.'

Everyone stopped work and gathered round the table in the middle of the hall. Gianni had her camera in one hand and was videoing her on his phone with the other.

It took a while, but finally she managed to remove the leather covering. Rather than the book she'd been expecting, it was a small, plain wooden casket with a brass lock. When she tried to open the lid, it refused to move. 'It's locked,' she said. And there was no key within the bundle.

'I'll go and see if the key's dropped out into the wall,' Robi said.

'What do you think's inside?' Gianni asked.

'Given the size, maybe papers or jewellery.' And then she caught her breath. A locked box, hidden under the floorboards of a cupboard by the water gate. As if someone had been planning a getaway and had stashed money or documents or… Her heart skipped a beat. Was this the proof of the family legend? Could this be Marianna's rubies?

Robi came back, shaking his head. 'Sorry. There's no key or anything in the cupboard or under it,' he said.

'Do you have any keys that might fit the lock?' Gianni asked.

'There are probably lots of old keys in the boxes on the fourth floor,' Serafina admitted, 'but finding one that fits is going to be like finding a needle in a haystack. Madi will probably know a specialist locksmith who can open it.' She wrinkled her nose. 'Though we might have to send it away.'

'In your shoes,' Gianni said, 'I'd want to know what's in that box as soon as possible—and I'd want to be there when it's opened.'

'My brother's a locksmith,' one of the construction workers said. 'If he can't open it, he'll know someone who can.'

'Could you ask him, please?' Serafina asked.

'Sure.' He took his phone out of his pocket and headed for a quieter area of the hall.

'What are you thinking?' Gianni asked when everyone had gone back to work.

'Why would you hide a locked box near a doorway?' she asked.

'It depends what's inside it. If it's money, then whoever put it there might have been planning some kind of secret escape.'

'Like eloping,' she said.

He looked at her. 'Marianna was going to elope. Do you think it's hers?'

'I'm trying not to get my hopes up,' she said. 'The box might be empty.'

'Rattle it,' he said.

She did, and there was definitely the sound of something moving.

'It could be coins,' he said.

'Or something else that could be turned into money.'

'Jewellery,' he said immediately.

She nodded. 'When Marianna's rubies went missing, everyone assumed they ended up at the bottom of the canal. But supposing she knew about the loose floorboard in the cupboard, and she'd hidden the box underneath it, intending to take her rubies with her to sell when she and her lover were far enough away?'

'Wouldn't she have worn her jewellery rather than hiding it?' Gianni asked.

'It'd be safer in a box,' Serafina said. 'Especially if she was trying to travel incognito. Say she'd borrowed a dress from one of her servants. Expensive jewellery pinned to a cheap dress would make people suspicious. Anyone who saw it might've thought she'd stolen it and they'd get a reward if they took her to the authorities, or they might've tried to steal it from her. Whereas if they were in a box like this, she could hide them safely in her dress.'

'If they are Marianna's rubies,' Gianni said, 'would they be worth a lot?'

'I studied fine art, not jewellery,' Serafina said. 'Your guess is as good as mine. But eighteenth-century jewellery is pretty rare. If they're the ones in Marianna's portrait, and they were found in this house and the plasterwork dates back far enough, it'd be provenance enough.'

The locksmith was there within the hour. Over a mug of coffee in Serafina's kitchen, he looked at the box. 'It's a simple tumbler lock. I'm pretty sure I can open it without damaging the box. If there's a problem, I'll stop, and we can look at your options.'

'Thank you,' she said.

'Nobody's seen what's inside this for decades, then?' the locksmith asked.

'Depending on what's in it, maybe for centuries,' Serafina said.

'It's a privilege to work on something like this,' he said. 'And it's a lot more interesting than my usual work of opening a door because someone's locked themselves out or a key's stuck.'

Serafina worked on her laptop while the locksmith worked on the lock.

Finally, he put his tools down. 'It's open. And, as it's your box, I think you should be the one to open it.'

'Gianni will want to see this, too,' she said. 'And your brother and the rest of the crew.'

They took the box downstairs, and Gianni called everyone round.

Serafina was aware of her heart beating faster—and not because of what she might find in the box. If they were Marianna's rubies, then she'd have the money to fund the restoration. Which meant that she and Gianni would be equals. And maybe, just maybe, they could have a future together.

The hinges of the box creaked as she opened it.

Inside, it was lined with black velvet.

Nestled in the velvet were a ruby choker, three bow-shaped brooches and a pair of earrings. Jewellery that she recognised instantly. 'They're the ones from Marianna's portrait,' she whispered.

The family rubies.

Everything that was once thought lost. And they had been in the house the whole time. Hidden, for hundreds of years.

Serafina's head swam, and she sat down. 'Poor Marianna.' Her eyes prickled with tears. 'All her hopes and dreams were in this box. A future with the man she loved. If only she hadn't tripped on the stairs.' She shook her head. 'That's so *sad*.'

Gianni squeezed her hand. 'I'm sorry.'

She blew out a breath. 'I need to tell my mother.'

'Of course. We'll all give you some space,' he said. 'Let me know if you need anything.'

'Thanks.' She closed the box, thanked the locksmith, and took the rubies up to her study before talking to her mother, her boss and her best friend.

Later that day, Maddalena came over with Enzo, a friend who worked at one of the other local museums and who specialised in jewellery. He handled the rubies carefully, checking them with a loupe. 'They're definitely eighteenth-century,' he said. 'Later jewellers could mimic the rose-cut, but if you look through the loupe you can see the tool-marks. They were cut by hand, not machine. It's why the stones aren't all identical.'

Serafina looked at the jewellery, seeing exactly what he meant, then handed the loupe to Gianni.

'The fastenings are all exactly what I'd expect from the early eighteenth century, and the stones are backed in gold rather than being openwork.' Enzo turned the largest brooch over to show them. 'Madi says you have provenance.'

'We found a cupboard in the wall when we were working on the restoration,' Gianni said. 'It had been blocked up from the inside of the house. The jewellery box was in a gap underneath the floor of the cupboard.' He showed the expert the photographs of the box in the wall.

'I didn't even know that cupboard existed. I've no idea how long the box has been there, though there's a family story that my great-however-many-times-aunt was trying to elope, three hundred years or so ago, except she fell down the stairs and broke her neck,' Serafina explained. 'I have a miniature of her.' She produced the portrait.

'That's incredible,' Enzo said, staring at the miniature and then the jewels. 'This is either the exact jewellery from the portrait, or an extremely good copy. Though I'd say these were original. And they're in incredible condition because they've been untouched for centuries. No damage, no repairs. I've never handled anything quite like this in all the years I've worked in a museum.'

'Can I ask a horrible question?' Serafina took a deep breath. 'Obviously I'd much rather lend these to a museum where they could be on show, along with Marianna's portrait—but, as you already know from Madi, the palazzo's currently being restored.'

'And restoration costs money,' Enzo said, catching on instantly. 'If you put them in an auction, what they'd fetch would depend on the day, but I can give you a ballpark estimate of their worth.' He named a sum that, had she not been sitting down, would've made Serafina fall over.

'It goes without saying, you need to keep them in a safe until you decide what to do with them.'

'We don't actually have a safe,' Serafina said. 'The family jewellery is all paste.'

'Except this,' Enzo said.

'The bank will be closed now. Do you want me to store the rubies in the museum's vault for you tonight?' Maddalena asked.

'Yes, please,' Serafina said gratefully.

'Let's go now,' Maddalena suggested.

'I'll leave you to it,' Gianni said. 'I have building works to oversee.'

'I…' Serafina knew she needed to say something. But all the words had gone out of her head. This was as much of a shock as learning that all the family money had gone and she was in debt. Now, she'd be able to repay the debt and pay Gianni on time. 'Thank you, Gianni. Without you…'

Gianni lifted one shoulder in a half-shrug and left.

'I'll come to the museum with you,' Enzo said. 'And I can give you the names of some good auction houses. The story of your great-aunt and how you found the rubies is going to raise a lot of interest. And I'll need to talk to our director. It's possible we might be able to make you an offer for the stones and the portrait, so they can stay in Venice.'

Serafina's head was whirring all the way to the

museum. Marianna's story had been the start of the downfall of Ca' d'Ardizzone. Maybe finding the rubies meant that the curse was lifted—and her relationship with Gianni stood a chance. She could pay for the repairs herself, instead of borrowing the money for the first stage from him. Meet him as his equal. She had her self-respect back.

And maybe, for the first time in centuries, an Ardizzone could be truly happy.

CHAPTER NINE

SERAFINA HADN'T ASKED him to go with her to the museum.

To Gianni, that felt like a bad sign.

On the one hand, maybe she'd see finding Marianna's rubies as a sign that the curse was lifted from her family.

On the other, selling the rubies meant that she'd be able to afford to pay for the renovations herself. She wouldn't need his help any more. And, even though he tried to tell himself that she wasn't like Elena's family and of course she wasn't going to back off from him, deep down he was scared that she'd see things differently now. That's she'd see the huge gap between their backgrounds and walk away.

By the time the stragglers on his team had left for the day, he still hadn't heard a thing from her.

She'd pushed him away. Shut him out.

How stupid he'd been to think that there was a chance things could work out between them.

His sister had been right, after all. He'd let his heart rule his head. Again.

Maybe it would be better to back off completely and leave one of his team in charge.

His stomach growled. He made himself a sandwich; but the food was tasteless.

By the time Serafina finally came back, he was in a foul mood.

'Sorry I was such a long time,' she said. 'Enzo had a lot of information for me. And the press officer at the museum wanted to talk to me to put a draft press release together. The story of Marianna and the rubies is going to help put the museum on the map when it moves here.'

'Uh-huh.' Though she still could've called. Or texted. Or *something*. The silence was what had upset him most.

She frowned. 'Are you all right?'

'Perfectly, thank you.'

She grimaced. 'Sorry. I should've called you to let you know I'd be a while.'

The fact that she hadn't stung more than he'd expected. 'I'm not your keeper,' he said. 'You don't have to tell me anything.'

She narrowed her eyes at him. 'That's uncalled for.'

He knew that, but he couldn't stop himself sniping. 'You're back to being *rich* little rich girl, then.'

She folded her arms. 'Looks like it. Surely that's a good thing, because it means you don't have to wait for me to pay your bills?'

Yes. And no. How could he tell her what was in his head? Especially when everything felt as if it had changed, and not for the better? That he thought she was rejecting him? And it brought back the way he'd felt when Elena had dumped him: that he wasn't good enough for her.

His silence made her narrow her eyes at him even more. 'Hang on. Are you angry because you're not my knight on a white charger any more?'

'No.' But she had a point, and it irritated him. He wasn't sure who he was more angry with—her, or himself.

'Oh, for pity's sake. *Men.*' She shook her head. 'I'm going to make dinner. Are you joining me?'

'I've already eaten.'

She lifted her chin. 'Right.'

He knew he was being rude. He could at least have a drink with her while she ate. But he didn't trust himself not to say something even more stupid. 'I have work to do. Excuse me.'

He thought she muttered something as she headed for the kitchen, but he wasn't going to ask her to repeat it. He knew pride was standing in his way; but he didn't want her to reject him, so it was better to avoid her until they'd both cooled down a bit. Wasn't it?

Except, the next morning, the tension between them felt worse. They barely spoke over breakfast. She went to the museum instead of working on the restoration, the way she usually did. And she avoided him in the evening on the grounds that she had a lot of admin to do and dinner was going to be a sandwich at her desk.

'I don't mind cooking for both of us,' he said, wanting to break the stalemate between them.

'I'm fine with a sandwich,' she said coolly.

She couldn't even accept a simple dinner from him?

If she wasn't going to meet him halfway, then they really weren't going to stand a chance.

Maybe absence would make the heart grow fonder. Or at least give him a chance to get his head straight and he could protect his heart. 'I'm going back to Rome tomorrow,' he said. 'I'm not sure when I'll be back. If you need anything, ask Robi.'

'OK,' she said.

She wasn't even going to wish him a safe journey?

Fine.

He booked the first train ticket he could get, left her a note the next morning with the keys to the back door and the water gate, suggesting that she could pass them on to Robi, the site manager, and headed back to Rome without seeing her.

Serafina stared at the note. Gianni hadn't even bothered to say goodbye in person. He'd simply left that cool little note next to the keys she'd given him.

Finding Marianna's rubies hadn't broken the Ardizzone curse, after all. She was as miserable now as she'd been when she'd broken up with Tom.

But at least she could fix the other problems in her life now. Her mother, the palazzo and the museum.

It would have to be enough.

She continued working with the restoration team during the day and doing her museum work in the evening. Although she knew that Gianni had been in contact with Robi every single day, for an update on the restoration, he hadn't left any message for her. She almost called him, several times, but each time she ended the call before it had even connected. She didn't have a clue what to say to him or how to get him to talk to her.

Weirdly, even though the palazzo was full of people, it felt emptier than the days she'd spent there alone. And she knew why: because Gianni wasn't there.

At the beginning of the following week, Enzo

had a meeting with her and the director of his own museum, and they made her a formal offer for the rubies. Although she knew she'd probably get more money if she put Marianna's jewellery up for auction, she wanted it to stay in Venice, so she accepted the offer.

As soon as the money came through, she paid a chunk off the taxes she owed, sent money to her mother, and did a bank transfer to Leto Construction.

Now the ball was in Gianni's court. He'd either talk to her or keep his distance: and his reaction would tell her how he really felt about her.

'Gi, there's something you need to see. Log in to the business bank account.' Flora leaned against her brother's desk.

Frowning, he did as she asked. There was a deposit from 'S Ardizzone'. A sum which covered everything up to the end of the first stage of renovations.

There was only one reason she could've afforded to pay him. 'She must have sold the rubies,' he said. And he damped down the hurt that she hadn't even bothered telling him what she was doing. She'd shut him out completely.

'You need to talk to her,' Flora said.

He shook his head. 'You were right in the first place. She doesn't need me any more.'

'If I were in her shoes,' Flora said, 'I'd hate having to ask for help. I'd hate having to be in someone's debt. Especially if it was someone I liked a lot.'

He said nothing.

Flora sighed. 'Gi, you're being stubborn. Obviously she likes you. Think about it. I know what happened with her ex. It was all over the gossip columns. That'd break anyone's ability to trust.'

He understood that. But he still hated the fact that Serafina had shut him out. He'd thought they were becoming a team, but she hadn't included him.

'I know Elena hurt you, but at least she didn't cheat on you. Imagine how hard it was for Serafina, walking in on her fiancé with someone else.'

He lifted one shoulder.

'Are you seriously going to let what happened with Elena wreck this for you, too?' Flora shook her head in exasperation.

'I thought you didn't like Serafina?'

'I didn't like the fact that you were bankrolling her,' Flora corrected. 'Yes, I worried at first that maybe you'd fallen for another Elena, but the fact she's paid you back like this tells me that she's not. That she's genuine. And you've got a chip on your shoulder, little brother. Just because she's posh, it doesn't mean she's going to hurt you.' She shook her head, looking exasperated.

'I'm half tempted to go and see Serafina myself, bring her back to Rome and bang your heads together. Sofia's got more sense than the pair of you combined.'

What was he meant to say to that?

Flora rolled her eyes. 'Stop being so stubborn. You miss her, don't you? And don't you *dare* do the strong-and-silent thing on me. Admitting your feelings is not a weakness.'

He sighed. 'Yes.' He hadn't been able to settle back in Rome. Home didn't feel like home any more, because she wasn't there.

'And I bet she misses you, too,' Flora said.

And that was his big fear. 'What if she doesn't?'

'She asked you for a three-month payment holiday, but she's paid the lot in one lump. That's a gesture, Gi. A big one. It means "Talk to me".'

'How do you know?'

'Because it's what I'd do in her shoes if I wanted you to talk to me.' Flora's voice gentled. 'And you've been like a bear with a sore head ever since you came back to Rome. Even Sofia says that Tio Gi is growly.'

He winced. 'Sorry.'

'Go and see her,' Flora said. 'You can't have a conversation like this on a phone or even a video call. It needs to be face-to-face.'

'I'm fine.'

Flora sighed and gave him a hug. 'At least think about it.'

'Uh-huh.'

'See you later, Growly.' But she looked sad rather than teasing.

Gianni fully intended to bury himself in paperwork.

Except he couldn't concentrate.

All he could think about was Serafina.

Was paying upfront a challenge, like Flora thought it was? Or was it Serafina's way of saying thank you and goodbye?

He picked up his phone and tapped on her name. And then he cut the call before it connected.

His sister had a point.

This ought to be a face-to-face conversation.

And there was a train to Venice in thirty minutes. He'd just about make it if he left the office now.

He went into his sister's office. 'I'm going to Venice.'

'Good.' She patted his shoulder. 'You know it makes sense.'

He missed the train.

The next one was a slow one.

He paced the platform until the next fast train arrived.

And then, once he'd boarded, the doubts came back. What if she wasn't there? She might have gone to see her mother. Or gone anywhere.

He should at least have phoned. Or maybe made an appointment with her.

Cross with himself, he called Maddalena. 'It's Gianni Leto. Do you happen to know where...?' What did he call her? The Contessa? Serafina?

'Serafina is?' Maddalena filled in. 'Yes. Right now, she's sitting at her desk in the office next door to mine. I'll transf—'

'No, please don't do that,' he cut in hastily.

Maddalena coughed. 'I'm not in the business of playing games, Signor Leto.'

'I'm not playing games. I'm on the train to Venice and I want to be sure she's there.'

'Wouldn't it have been better to check *before* you got on the train?'

He knew he deserved every bit of the 'How stupid are you?' tone. 'I wasn't completely sure she'd speak to me. We...um...had a slight falling-out before I left.'

'If you hurt her,' Maddalena said, her voice dangerously calm, 'I'll come after you and cut out your heart with my letter-opener. Which is blunt, so it will take a long and painful time.'

'I'm not going to hurt her,' Gianni said. 'But if you can keep her at the office until I get there, I'd appreciate it.'

For a moment, he thought she was going to refuse. But then she sighed. 'All right. I'll keep her here.'

The rest of the journey felt as if it took for ever, but at last the train crossed the causeway and he could see the city rising out of the sea.

He caught the *vaporetto* to the Accademia, then got out his phone to make sure he was heading in the right direction through the narrow alleyways to the Museum of Women's Art. On the way, he passed a florist's.

Should he take Serafina flowers?

He owed her a lot more than flowers. He owed her honesty.

But flowers might help break the ice a little.

Then he realised he didn't have a clue what her favourite flowers were. Roses felt too cliched. But then he saw a bucket full of sunflowers, and they made him think of her. How he felt when he was with her: as if the world was bright and shiny and new.

He bought a large bunch, then found his way to the museum. The receptionist was one of the people who'd given up her spare time to work on the palazzo; recognising him, she smiled. 'Are you here to see Serafina?'

'If she's in her office, yes.'

'I'll just c—'

'Please don't,' he said. 'I want to surprise her.'

The receptionist looked at the flowers. 'OK. I'll buzz you through.'

She directed him through the back to the museum offices, and he rapped on Serafina's open door.

'Come i—' She lifted her head and stopped mid-sentence when she saw him.

'I brought you these,' he said, lifting the sunflowers.

She made no move to take them. 'Why?'

'Because...' He blew out a breath and closed the door behind him. 'Because I don't know what to say to you. I've spent three hours on a train, trying to plan what to say, and nothing sounds right. And I saw these on the way here, and I thought you'd like them, and they remind me of you because they're like sunshine, and I thought they might break the ice, and—' He stopped and groaned. 'I'm babbling like an idiot.'

'You are.' But she was smiling. 'Thank you. They're lovely.'

'We need to talk,' he said.

'Not here. Let's go for a walk,' she said. 'I'll put these in water in the kitchen and let Madi know I'm going out.'

He nodded and waited in the doorway to her office while she went to the kitchen.

'Madi, I'm leaving my desk for a bit,' she said.

'My fault,' Gianni said, leaning round the doorway.

Maddalena smiled, waved her letter-opener at him and did an elaborate wink.

'What was that about?' Serafina asked as she led Gianni out of the museum.

'She was reminding me of our conversation this morning, when I asked her to keep you here. She said if I hurt you, she'll cut out my heart with her letter-opener.'

Serafina grinned. 'And she would. She's scary, our Madi.'

'She is,' he said.

He waited until they'd left the museum and found an empty bench on the wide pavement overlooking the canal before speaking again.

'I'm sorry,' he said. 'I've been very stupid.'

He waited for her to agree. Or at least say something.

Eventually, she sighed. 'You're not the only one.'

Relief flooded through him. At least she recognised they were both at fault. 'Thank you for the stage payment. Which I note is a couple of months earlier than we agreed.'

'Because I sold the rubies to Enzo's museum. I'm loaning him Marianna's portrait, on condition we get to display the rubies for the first six months when our museum opens at the palazzo.'

'That sounds good.' Except it wasn't the rubies or Marianna he wanted to know about. It was Serafina. 'How are you?'

'Perfectly fine, thank you. And you?'

He could be polite back; or he could be the first to admit the truth.

'Miserable,' he said.

He held her gaze. Would she admit how she felt, too? Or would she push him away?

Her shoulders drooped. 'Me, too.'

'I missed you,' he said softly.

'Did you? Because you left without even saying goodbye.'

'Because I was angry and hurt,' he said. 'As well as thoroughly in the wrong. What you said about me wanting to be a knight on a white charger—that was all true.'

'And I pushed you away because I panicked,' she said. 'Relationships don't work, in my family.'

'I know. The curse. But haven't you broken it, now? You found the rubies, you're telling Marianna's story to the world, and you're rescuing the palazzo.' He looked at her. 'And you sent me the money.'

'I didn't want to be beholden to you,' she said. 'I wanted to fix things myself. So I can meet you as your equal.'

He frowned. 'My *equal*? Hang on. You're a *contessa*. That makes you way, way above my station.'

She scoffed. 'Who cares?'

'I wasn't good enough for Elena's family. And you're really posh. What makes me good enough for yours?' he asked.

'You're good enough because you're you,' she said simply, and took his hand. 'I'm not Elena, and you're not Tom.'

He squeezed her hand. 'I'd never cheat on you.'

'And I'd never look down on you.'

'What, exactly,' he asked, 'are we both worrying about?'

'That it's going to go wrong and we'll get hurt,' she said.

'If we talk, if we're honest with each other—there might be times when we fall out and start fighting, but if we trust each other instead of trying to second-guess each other we'll get through the sticky spots,' he said. 'It's *not* talking that makes things go wrong.'

'The palazzo's felt empty without you,' she said.

He coughed. 'Are you telling me our crew stopped working when I went back to Rome?'

'No. Just it *felt* empty,' she said.

'Rome doesn't feel like home any more,' he said.

She was silent for such a long time that he didn't think she was going to answer. But then her voice cracked slightly as she asked, 'Could Venice be home?'

'I think,' he said, 'home might be where you are.'

Her eyes glittered with tears. 'That's the nicest thing anyone's ever said to me.'

'I mean it. I want to be with you, Serafina. I want to make a future with you. Make a family with you.' He looked at her. 'But that all rather depends on what you want.'

'I want to be with you, too,' she said. 'A future and a family sounds perfect.' She paused. 'I'm sorry I panicked and pushed you away.'

'I'm sorry I pushed you away, too,' he said.

'We're both in the wrong,' she said.

'Then let's make it right,' Gianni said. He cupped her cheek with his hand. 'When you asked me to come here, you showed me *your* Venice. But it wasn't the city I fell in love with. It was you. And I was furious when you asked me to marry you, because I didn't want a marriage of convenience. I don't want to walk away from you after a year. I don't want to walk away from you, ever. I want you for a lifetime. I love you.'

'I love you, too,' she said.

He brushed his mouth lightly against hers. 'Will you marry me—not for the palazzo, but for me?'

'Yes.'

'Then let's seal the deal,' he said, and kissed her.

EPILOGUE

Two years later

GIANNI STEERED HIS wife out of the front door. 'Stop worrying. Marianna's going to be fine.'

'I guess having six babysitters for our first night out without our daughter might seem a bit over the top,' Serafina said.

He shook his head. 'Best compromise ever,' he said. 'Neither of our mums wanted to miss out on being her first babysitter. Neither did your Tia Vittoria or my sister.'

'And Lessi and Madi staked their claim as her godmothers,' Serafina said. 'You're right. Best compromise ever.'

'Plus it means,' he said, 'we get time on our own.'

'Are you sure you don't want that lobster in a Michelin-starred restaurant? It's been two years, now, and I still haven't made good on that promise,' Serafina reminded him.

He grinned. 'I've got a much better idea. *Cichéti,*

catch of the day in our favourite *osteria*, and then dancing in the moonlight in St Mark's Square.' He spun her into his arms for a kiss. 'And then I'm going to kiss you and tell you how much I love you on every single bridge on the way home.'

She laughed. 'That sounds perfect. And, with six babysitters, we can take the long way home…'

* * * * *

*If you enjoyed this story,
check out these other great reads from
Kate Hardy*

Finding Mr Right in Florence
Soldier Prince's Secret Baby
Surprise Heir for the Princess
Snowbound with the Brooding Billionaire

All available now!